THE ZUCCHINI WARRIORS

THE ZUCCHINI WARRIORS

GORDON KORMAN

**SCHOLASTIC
HARDCOVER**

Scholastic Inc.
New York

LIBRARY OF CONGRESS
Library of Congress Cataloging-in-Publication Data

Korman, Gordon.
The Zucchini Warriors / Gordon Korman.
p.   cm.
Summary: Roommates Bruno and Boots find obstacles in their way as they attempt to lead the Macdonald Hall Zucchini Warriors to a victorious football season and earn the reward of a new recreation center.

ISBN 0-590-41335-X

[1. Football — Fiction.   2. Schools — Fiction.]   I. Title.
PZ7.K8369Zu   1988
[Fic] — dc19
                                                              88-6720
                                                                CIP
                                                                 AC

12 11 10 9 8 7 6 5 4 3 2 1   8 9/8 0 1 2 3/9

Printed in the U.S.A.   12

First Scholastic printing, September 1988

For Elaine Blankenship,
who hates football and likes zucchini sticks.
I forgive you.

Contents

1.
Hank
the
Tank

A lone figure stood beneath the tall scoreboard, arms crossed, glaring. The Macdonald Hall football stadium, brand-new and immaculate, stretched before him, taking up most of the large lawn north of the Faculty Building. Frowning, Bruno Walton sat down in the first row of bleachers.

"Hey, Bruno!" Boots O'Neal came sprinting across the campus from the direction of the dormitories. He pulled to a stop in front of his longtime roommate and friend, and held out his hand. "How was your summer?"

Bruno didn't seem to notice the greeting. "Well," he said, shaking his head, "somebody really blew it this time. I mean, what is this?"

1

"It's a football field," said Boots. "What do you think it is?"

"I know what it is, and it isn't what it's supposed to be. We put in for a rec hall, remember?"

Boots sighed. "Bruno, when a guy gives big money to a school, he has the right to say what it's going to be used for. Be happy. This is a great stadium. Look at that scoreboard. I bet even the pro teams don't have a better one."

"We made a formal proposal," said Bruno steadily. "This Carson guy gave the money to the school. *We're* the school."

"We're two guys," Boots amended.

"We handed in a petition with hundreds of names," said Bruno hotly.

"And we wrote every single one of them," Boots added.

"It took us *all night*! It's not easy making those signatures look different. Besides, there's no way The Fish could know we did it."

"Not unless he read the names and tried to find Godzilla McMurphy on the student list."

"Look," said Bruno in exasperation, "we couldn't be expected to remember the names of seven hundred guys. We're the victims, Boots! They took our rec hall money and built the Rose Bowl! We don't even have a football team! When The Fish hears about this, heads will roll!"

Boots had to laugh. "The Fish notices when your grades go down two percent. He probably already knows there's a football stadium outside his office window. Come on, Bruno. We haven't seen each other for two months. Hello. How are you?"

2

Finally Bruno grinned sheepishly, and the two shook hands. "Sorry. It's just that I was planning to lounge out in the rec hall tonight, maybe play a couple of games of Ping-Pong, and watch some tube on the wide-screen TV. This is quite a shock, Boots!"

Boots pointed to the three large duffle bags sitting by the 40-yard line. "Let me guess. You got right off the bus and came here. You didn't even take your stuff to our room. Here, I'll give you a hand." He walked over to the field and slung one bag over his shoulder.

Bruno picked up the other two, but dropped them immediately, his face wreathed in smiles. "Look!" He pointed to a second-story window in the Faculty Building. "There's The Fish! He still looks pretty good for such an old guy."

"He looks like he always looks," said Boots, "like he's putting someone on dishwashing duty for fifty years." He gazed nervously up to the window at William R. Sturgeon, Headmaster of Macdonald Hall. Even from a distance he could make out the steely gray eyes. The Headmaster's nickname, The Fish, was more than just a play on his name, because when Mr. Sturgeon looked at a boy through his metal-rimmed spectacles, it was a cold, fishy stare. Boots had been on the receiving end of that look too many times.

"Come on, Boots. The Fish is almost like a buddy of ours after all we've been through together. Why, I'll bet he's spent more time with us than any other guys in the whole school."

"That's because we're in trouble more than any other guys in the whole school. Bruno, this can be the year where we see as little of our buddy The Fish as possible. We keep our noses clean and have a great time."

But his words were wasted on Bruno's receding back. Bruno stepped up to the base of the building, cupped his hands to his mouth, and called, "Hello, sir! Down here!"

Mr. Sturgeon's head emerged from the second-floor window. The Headmaster regarded Bruno and then Boots a cautious distance behind him. "Good day, Walton — O'Neal. Welcome back."

There was an uncomfortable pause. "So, Mr. Sturgeon — " Bruno began. "What's new?"

"The staff and I are looking forward to the up-coming academic year," the Headmaster replied briskly. "And no doubt you have noticed our new football facility. It is quite outstanding. Now, if you boys don't mind, there are many things to which I must attend."

"Well, there *is* one thing Boots — uh, Melvin — and I are concerned about. Sir, do you remember the petition we gave you last year along with the plan for our new rec hall?"

"I certainly do," Mr. Sturgeon called down sternly. "It was with great surprise that I discovered that Napoleon Bonaparte is a registered student at Macdonald Hall. I don't suppose you boys considered that falsifying signatures is illegal — even if most of the signatories are deceased."

"We're sorry," Boots shuffled.

"Well, how about the plan?" Bruno persisted.

The Headmaster suppressed a smile. "A trifle elaborate, don't you think? Particularly the wave pool and the spiral staircase."

4

Bruno shrugged. "All right. We can lose the staircase."

"Walton, Mr. Carson's endowment has already been spent. You will be informed all about it at the opening assembly tomorrow morning. Good day." He shut the window, indicating the interview was over.

"Nice going," Boots commented. "You haven't been here forty-five minutes, and already we've been chewed out by The Fish."

Bruno folded his arms in front of him. "You know, The Fish is a good Headmaster, but sometimes he can get on a guy's nerves. 'Already been spent'!"

The opening assembly was delayed because Sidney Rampulsky fell down the Faculty Building stairs.

"Give him air!" Bruno shouted, standing over Sidney.

Boots came running onto the scene with a wet towelette from the washroom, and applied it to Sidney's forehead.

Gingerly Sidney sat up and focused on the crowd of boys regarding him intently. "What's everybody staring at? Haven't you ever seen a guy fall down the stairs before?"

"You're such a klutz!" stormed Mark Davies, Sidney's roommate.

Bruno shook his head. "That's not it. This is an annual event. Sidney always takes a spill before the opening assembly. Remember the time he came in the stage door and tripped over The Fish's chair with The Fish still in it?"

"It's a tradition," agreed Pete Anderson, nodding wisely.

Bruno grabbed Sidney's arm and helped him to his feet. "Come on, guys. The sooner we get the assembly started, the sooner we can get to the bottom of this football business and start figuring out a way to get our rec hall back."

"Back?" repeated studious Elmer Drimsdale, his confused expression magnified by his thick horn-rimmed glasses. "Our recreational facility never existed, so how could we possibly get it back?"

"The rec hall came into existence when Boots and I drew up the proposal," said Bruno righteously.

"Only according to you," Boots amended.

"In the hearts and minds of the students of Macdonald Hall!" Bruno exclaimed. "And it was taken away when they built that monstrosity on the north lawn!"

Pete was mystified. "I think it's great that we're going to have a football team. Aren't you going to try out?"

"Never!" Bruno thundered. "That would be a nail in our rec hall's coffin!"

The auditorium was already full as they filed in and took their seats. Bruno tuned out Mr. Sturgeon's welcoming speech, since he'd heard it several times before. He perked up, though, at the very first mention of the football stadium and its donor, Mr. Henry Carson.

"Mr. Carson graduated from Macdonald Hall in 1958," Mr. Sturgeon was saying, "and went on to become a professional athlete. Perhaps you are familiar with his football nickname" — he grimaced with distaste — "Hank the Tank."

There was a murmur through the crowd.

"That's Hank the Tank Carson!" whispered Pete excitedly. "From the Green Bay Packers! Wow!"

"Since his retirement from football, he has become a very successful businessman," the Headmaster went on. "No doubt you have seen his popular Mr. Zucchini snack wagons."

A buzz of recognition shaded with amusement swept through the students. Bruno looked impressed.

"Hank the Tank is Mr. Zucchini? Far out!"

"Have you ever tried those deep-fried zucchini sticks?" Boots whispered.

"Of course not. Have you?"

"Of course not."

Mr. Sturgeon cleared his throat. "Boys, please show your gratitude to Mr. Henry Carson."

Henry Carson was one of those men who had once been broad and muscular, but had become flabby as his business responsibilities left him less and less time for exercise. His massive shoulders and solid frame explained his connection with football. Below them, his considerable potbelly indicated his involvement with the food business. His long legs took him to the podium in a single stride, and he looked out over the assembled boys and grinned broadly.

"Good morning, men. I'm Hank the Tank Carson, and I'm talking football. Are you up for it?"

There was a smattering of lukewarm applause.

Carson scowled. "Come on, men — what *is* this — Macdonald Hall, or Joe Shmoe's School? Let's hear it!"

In the embarrassed silence that followed, Bruno leaped to his feet. "Mr. Carson, we're all really grateful for the football stadium, but — uh — a rec hall was — "

Mr. Sturgeon stood up. "Walton, that will do."

"But sir," Bruno persisted, fighting off Boots, who was attempting to pull him back down into his seat. "I'm speaking on behalf of the students — "

"That's enough, Walton. This outbreak is childish and rude, and unworthy — "

"Wait a minute," Mr. Carson interrupted. He looked down at Bruno. "What's all this about a rec hall?"

"Well, Mr. Carson, the students were all hoping to get one. Nothing spectacular, you understand. Just a place to hang out. You know — couches, TV, maybe a Ping-Pong table or two. . . ."

Mr. Carson smiled broadly. "I'll make you a deal. We'll put together a football team and work real hard. And if our team makes a good showing, I'll see to it that you get the best rec hall you can imagine!"

"Three cheers for Mr. Carson!" shouted Bruno delightedly.

The auditorium rocked with three resounding "hip hip hoorays" from over seven hundred throats.

Henry Carson was positively glowing. "Tryouts are tomorrow at three-thirty, so don't work yourselves too hard in classes. Tell your teachers Hank the Tank says it's okay. And now, men, I've arranged for a special treat — "

Suddenly the sound of bells filled the auditorium. The boys all looked around in confusion as the ringing grew louder, until the main doors opened wide, and in rode eight bicycle-driven Mr. Zucchini snack wagons.

"*Zucchini sticks for everybody!*" bellowed Mr. Carson, expecting the trucks to be mobbed by ecstatic students. Instead, an embarrassed hum went up.

"Zucchini sticks?"

"They want us to *eat* zucchini sticks?"

"Yeccch!"

"Do they come in chocolate?"

"What's a zucchini?"

"Don't be shy," coaxed Mr. Carson. "First come, first served."

Bruno was making his way through the crowd, dragging Boots with one arm and Elmer with the other.

"Aw, Bruno," moaned Boots, "why do we have to eat those dumb zucchini sticks? No one else is."

"Think of our rec hall," said Bruno. "We can't insult Hank the Tank."

"Deep-fried foodstuffs are bad for the cardiovascular system," complained Elmer. "And the nutritional value of the zucchini is greatly diminished by the frying process. The batter is dangerously high in cholesterol, and — "

"Stow it, Elm," interrupted Bruno. "Where's your school spirit?" He walked up to the nearest wagon and dutifully received a small plate piled high with batter-fried spears about three inches long.

"Sweet-and-Sour sauce, Blue Cheese, or Hot Mustard?" inquired the vendor.

"Blue Cheese." He accepted a small cup of dressing and handed it, along with the zucchini sticks, to Boots. "Eat," he ordered.

"Me? Why me?"

"Eat."

Miserably Boots dipped his first zucchini stick into the sauce just deep enough to leave a tiny speck of blue cheese dressing on the batter coating. He put it in his mouth and chewed gingerly, holding his breath to mask the taste.

"Hey, everybody," Bruno announced. "Boots loves them! He says they taste like French fries, only a thousand times better!"

Instantly students began converging on the eight trucks, to the great delight of Bruno and Mr. Carson.

"Mildred, thirty years ago my least favorite student graduated from Macdonald Hall," said Mr. Sturgeon to his wife over tea that afternoon. "And today he is back to haunt me by turning my entire school into a farm team for the Dallas Cowboys."

"Yes, yes, you've been complaining about Henry Carson all summer," she said.

The Headmaster took a long drink from his cup. "He was an obnoxious boy who has bloomed into an obnoxious man. Do you know what he had the nerve to do? He paraded in a convoy of those awful Mr. Zucchini wagons, and goaded our boys into tasting his wares." He chuckled in spite of himself. "Poor O'Neal was the first to try one. I thought he was going to keel over dead."

"Melvin!" Mrs. Sturgeon exclaimed, clasping her hands in front of her. "A lovely boy. His friend Bruno is back as well, I hope?"

"Walton's here. And I might add that his timing is as good as ever. He interrupted Carson's speech."

"How rude! What happened?"

Mr. Sturgeon looked disgusted. "Carson promised the students the recreation hall they've been petitioning for if they go along with him and form a football team. It sounded suspiciously like a bribe to me."

His wife sighed. "Dear, it's been thirty years since Henry graduated. Isn't it time to forgive and forget?"

"Never," the Headmaster replied savagely. "He compromised my principles as a teacher. I passed that boy in Algebra, even though he *failed*. I added marks to his score because he spelled his name right!"

"Well, that's your flaw, not his," she contended.

"I had no choice, Mildred. If I'd kept him from graduating, he'd have been *back*. I couldn't have tolerated another year of Carson. I'd have given up teaching. If I'd failed him, I'd be a delicatessen man today, slicing bologna."

"William, you're getting all worked up about nothing."

"Maybe," he replied. "But I refuse to allow Henry Carson and his football to compromise the academic standards of Macdonald Hall!"

At a corner table in the dining hall, nine boys enjoyed their last dinner before the onset of classes the next morning.

"Boots, I'm pretty ticked off at you!" exclaimed Pete Anderson. "Those zucchini sticks aren't better than French fries! I almost threw up!"

A babble of protest arose as each boy related his own opinion of Mr. Carson's zucchini sticks. The votes were in at 9–0 against. Even Wilbur Hackenschleimer, Macdonald Hall's champion eater, looked up from his meat loaf to make a sour face at the mention of Mr. Zucchini.

"It's all for a good cause," Bruno explained. "When our football team starts burning up the league, he's going to fork over our rec hall."

"Listen, Bruno," said Boots. "None of us knows beans about football. We've never played in an organized game, with refs, and rules, and all that stuff. Even if we turn out to be pretty good, you've seen the killers that play on high school and college teams. They're fantastic!"

"But we won't be going against high school and college killers. We'll be playing against guys at *our level*. I want to see *everybody* at those tryouts tomorrow."

"Not me," mumbled big Wilbur from behind a mountain of mashed potatoes. "I'm not getting out on the field with a bunch of huge monster gorillas."

"*You're* a huge monster gorilla," pointed out Larry Wilson, his roommate.

"Tell all the guys," said Bruno. "I want to see every ounce of talent we've got out on that field tomorrow."

It was after three in the morning when Boots was awakened by a loud noise at the window of room 306 in Dormitory 3. He sat up in bed and looked over at Bruno, who was fast asleep, snoring full tilt.

Crack!

A rock the size of a hardball came sailing out of nowhere and hit the window loudly. Boots scrambled out of bed and looked outside, but could see nothing except two sizable cracks in the glass. Suddenly a familiar head bobbed into view. Boots opened the latch and helped in Cathy Burton and Diane Grant, old friends from Miss Scrimmage's Finishing School for Young Ladies, located directly across the highway from Macdonald Hall.

After greetings were exchanged, Cathy examined her surroundings. "Same old room." She motioned towards the snoring Bruno. "Same old buzz saw." Casually she switched on the portable radio next to Bruno's bed and turned the volume up to full.

Bruno shot bolt upright. "What? What?"

Boots dove for the off switch. "Cathy, are you crazy?" he hissed. "Do you want Mr. Fudge on our necks?"

In the hall, they heard the Housemaster's door open, followed by Mr. Fudge's footsteps. He paused and, finding all quiet, returned to his room.

"Sorry," grinned Cathy. "I just figured you guys needed some liveliness around here. You know, we were expecting you to stop by tonight."

Bruno shook his head. "We're in training."

"For what?" asked Diane.

"Football!" declared Bruno, as though the new Macdonald Hall team had been announced on *World News Tonight* and everyone should know about it.

"But you don't have a football team," Diane pointed out.

"Sure, not today. But tomorrow we will. I can hardly wait to get out there with the old hog's hide."

"Pigskin," Cathy corrected.

"Whatever," said Bruno. "Listen. Here's the

story." He outlined the history of Mr. Carson's endowment to the school and his promise regarding the rec hall.

"You're planning to have a winning team in your first year?" Cathy asked incredulously.

"We've got one thing on our side," said Boots sarcastically. "The pushiest guy in Ontario." He pointed to Bruno.

"Cathy used to play a lot of football," put in Diane. "With her three brothers. Right, Cathy?"

"Well," Bruno chuckled, "football is really a man's game — no offense, girls. You can be, you know, cheerleaders or something."

Cathy wound up and swatted him on the side of the head.

"Hey!" bawled Bruno. "What was that for?"

"Come on, Diane," said Cathy, opening the window. "Let's get out of here." The two girls exited in a huff.

"What's eating them?" mused Boots.

Bruno shrugged. "That was weird." He climbed back into bed, and was snoring again in seconds.

Brow knit, Boots lay down. It took him over an hour to get back to sleep.

2.
An
Endangered
Species

On a flat section of roof atop Miss Scrimmage's Finishing School for Young Ladies perched Cathy Burton and Diane Grant. Cathy was gazing through a pair of high-powered field binoculars, watching the Macdonald Hall football tryouts with great interest.

"Cathy, are you sure Miss Scrimmage didn't see us sneak out of her 'manners' lecture?"

Cathy didn't hear her. "They stink!" she exclaimed in disgust. "These guys know nothing about football! They've got *Boots* at quarterback. And look — Sidney Rampulsky at wide receiver!"

"It's only the first day," Diane argued lamely.

"Wait a minute! Sidney caught it! And look at him go! He can really run! Come on, Sidney — whoops!" She looked away from the binoculars.

15

"That's the first time I've ever seen someone trip over the 30-yard line!"

"Is he okay?" Diane asked.

Cathy peered through the glasses again. "I can't tell. I guess so. Ah, wait a minute — Bruno's going to kick a field goal."

"I didn't know he could kick," said Diane.

Cathy snorted. "He can't. He got it about four feet off the ground. It hit somebody in the stomach. Hey, it's Wilbur Hackenschleimer! He's chasing Bruno around the field. Bruno's running — no, he's hiding behind Boots. There's a lot of pushing going on. Hold it. There's a guy in a suit. It's — " She looked at Diane. "Hey, wow. It's Mr. Sturgeon."

"We are instituting a football program," lectured the Headmaster, "not an excuse to brawl. Walton, Hackenschleimer, what do you have to say for yourselves?"

Mr. Carson came to their aid. "The men are just high-spirited from the practice . . ." he began.

Mr. Sturgeon faced him with a fishy stare. "They will learn to control their high spirits, or there will be no more practices."

"But the board of directors — "

"Expects me to maintain discipline at Macdonald Hall," finished Mr. Sturgeon firmly.

Mr. Carson studied the grass. "Yes, Mr. Sturgeon."

Bruno let his breath out as the Headmaster walked off in the direction of the Faculty Building. "Thanks a lot, Mr. Carson. You saved our lives!"

The former student smiled. "I know what it feels like to be chewed out by The Fish."

Pete Anderson was awed. "You know about that? I mean that he's — ?"

"The Fish? Of course. Listen, I don't want you men to think of me as a teacher. I want to be one of the guys. And together we're going to build a great team. Although," he added less enthusiastically, "we're going to need a lot of work."

"That bad, eh?" said Wilbur.

Mr. Carson nodded. "But I'll have you men whipped into shape in no time." He stepped back and cupped his hands to his mouth so that all the boys could hear. "All right, everybody! Thanks for coming out! The list of who made it will be posted outside the gym as soon as I make my decisions!" Coach Flynn shot him a dirty look, so he added, "And Mr. Flynn here, of course. But don't hit the showers yet, because dinner's on me!"

Bruno started to say, "Three cheers for Mr. Carson," but then he heard bells.

"Zucchini sticks for everybody!" exclaimed Mr. Carson, as the wagons filed in behind the bleachers via a service driveway.

"This is cruel," Sidney observed miserably.

"Look," said Larry. "He's a grown man. He's not going to die if we don't eat his zucchini sticks. He can take it."

"No," said Bruno firmly. "We can't offend Hank the Tank."

"Bruno, don't you think it's a little selfish to act phony to this guy just because we want a rec hall?" challenged Boots.

"It's more than that," said Bruno. "You saw how he defended me and Wilbur in front of The Fish. Hank the Tank is *us* in thirty years!"

17

"I don't intend to have the potbelly," said Boots.

"I do," put in Wilbur. "But it isn't going to come from zucchini sticks. Peanut butter, yes — and maybe a little pasta. . . ."

"The Tank is really keen on the honor of Macdonald Hall," Bruno went on, the orator in him swinging into full gear. "Well, he's right. We have to show the other schools in this province that we can take a sport we know nothing about, and put together a great team. Okay, so today's practice didn't go so hot; okay, we have to gag down a few zucchini sticks — do we give up this easily on the honor of Macdonald Hall?"

"When you put it that way," said Mark Davies slowly, "I guess we owe it to the Hall to do our best."

"I'm with you," said Larry.

The other boys present all murmured their assent.

Boots looked half amused and half disgusted. "All right, Bruno, you've done it again. You've convinced everybody. What do you want us to do first?"

Bruno smiled engagingly. "The first thing we do is get over to the wagons and pig out on those zucchini sticks!"

"I don't get it," said Boots, scrambling to keep up with Bruno, who was striding purposefully down the hallway of Dormitory 2. "Why do we have to see Elmer Drimsdale?"

"With Hank the Tank on our side, and the football team in motion and bound for greatness," Bruno replied, "we're going to be up for a rec hall soon. We can't take any chances. We're going to the smartest guy in the school to get the perfect layout."

"Why do we have to submit a plan at all?" asked Boots.

"Because if we don't tell them exactly what we want, they'll build us the kind of thing *they* want us to have." He rapped sharply at the door of room 201. "Hi, Elm. It's us."

Bruno kicked the door, and the two boys stepped inside. Both Bruno and Boots had once been roommates of Elmer's, but each time they entered his living space there was cause to gawk afresh. Elmer was a one-man research and development team for everything, and the small dormitory room was completely cluttered with experiments and inventions. Books were piled everywhere, with rare potted plants on top of the stacks. A complete chemistry laboratory dominated the left side of the room, forcing Elmer's formidable collection of computers and electronic gadgetry to the right. And tools, coils of wire, voltage meters, microscopes, and crystals were piled in and around the ant farm and the fish tank. On the walls were various charts and graphs of ongoing experiments, and a large labeled diagram of the Pacific salmon, Elmer's pride and joy.

"Oh, hello." Elmer appeared in the bathroom doorway. "What can I do for you?"

"Elmer. Just the man I wanted to see," said Bruno. "We need you to help us with the new floor plan for the rec hall."

"But I understood that the new facility will be constructed only when the football team begins to meet with some success," Elmer protested.

"In other words, soon," said Bruno. "So see what you can come up with. The Fish dumped all over

19

our last plan. I think he hates staircases. Maybe we should go for a one floor, ranch-style layout." He looked thoughtful, and mused, "Then how would we get in the scenic overview?"

Suddenly Boots's sharp eyes detected some movement by the base of the disk drive, and he grabbed Bruno's shoulder. "Look!"

"A rat!" Bruno exclaimed. "They've got rats in Dormitory 2!"

"No!" Elmer bent down and picked up a small gray-brown creature. "It's my latest experiment."

"Experiment?!" chorused Bruno and Boots in horror.

"You're not going to — like — *dissect* it or anything?" Bruno added.

"Of course not," said Elmer, highly insulted. "This is a Manchurian bush hamster, a rare species descended from both the cat and rodent families."

Both boys stared. The Manchurian bush hamster was about the size of a kitten only thinner, with shorter fur all over its body, except for the neck. There the hair was long and stiff, forming an elaborate frame for the small head.

"Well, what *are* you going to do with it?" asked Boots.

"The Manchurian bush hamster is in danger of becoming extinct," lectured Elmer. "They breed very seldom, and no one knows how to make them reproduce more frequently. If an answer can't be found soon, I'm afraid we might lose the whole species."

Bruno brightened. "Well, those bush hamsters' troubles are over if you're on the case, Elm. You'll figure it out no sweat."

spirit! I nominate you for captain! Okay, men?"

The group cheered its approval.

"And I pick Boots O'Neal as co-captain!" Bruno added joyfully.

Boots tried to decline the honor, but his frantic signaling was ignored by his raucous teammates. He glared at Bruno.

Henry Carson was glowing pink with pleasure. "All right, men! The football season is now officially on! I want you out on that field all suited up every day after classes — starting tomorrow!"

"Even in bad weather?" asked Wilbur timidly.

"The Beast loves bad weather!" Calvin snarled. "You can be meaner in mud!"

In the midst of the excitement, Mr. Carson threw open his front door to reveal two Mr. Zucchini wagons, bells ringing. "Snack time!"

The jubilation died instantly.

"Oh, wow," said Bruno into the painful silence. "Zucchini sticks. I just can't get enough of that Blue Cheese Dressing."

"Come and get it!" crowed Carson.

But still the group hung back, until Larry Wilson was struck with inspiration. "Fan-tastic!" he exclaimed. "But I'm still stuffed from dinner. So I'll take mine 'to go.' I'm always starving by lights-out."

"Me, too!" chorused twenty-five other throats.

"Great idea!" bawled Carson. "They're delicious cold, too. Help yourselves, men. And I'll see you on the field!"

Walking back from the guest cottage, the boys had nothing but praise for Larry.

"Man, you saved our lives!" exclaimed Dave.

"Yeah," Pete agreed. "Elmer might have to step

down as school genius. Quick — where's the nearest garbage can?"

"What are you — nuts?" Bruno stopped the procession. "Don't let me see anybody throwing out those zucchini sticks. If Hank the Tank sees them in the garbage, it'll break his heart!"

"Better his heart than my stomach," said Wilbur feelingly.

"Bruno, I really don't think Mr. Carson goes through the trash cans."

"We can't take the chance — partly for our rec hall, but mostly because Hank the Tank is a great guy."

"Well, what are we supposed to do with them?" Wilbur challenged. "Eat them?"

Bruno grinned, his dark eyes gleaming. "Of course not. We can't throw them out, but we can give them a burial at sea — flush the evidence."

It was a very merry football team that made its way back to the three dormitories that evening.

"Why so quiet, Boots?" Bruno asked as the two entered room 306. "You haven't said anything since the meeting."

"Bruno, there are no words to describe how much I want to wring your neck!"

Bruno looked amazed. "Why?"

"Up until tonight," his roommate said accusingly, "our noses were completely clean. Sure, you were bugging The Fish the first day, and you opened your mouth at the assembly — that's nothing. But now you've made us captains of the football team, which means that when something goes wrong with the Zucchini Warriors, The Fish is going to come to *us*."

Bruno laughed. "You know what your problem is? You worry too much, and about the wrong things. Why are you thinking about problems that don't even exist when you should be thinking about how we're going to get two jumbo orders of zucchini sticks down the toilet?" He hefted the two plates and switched on the bathroom light. "Grab the Blue Cheese Dressing, Melvin. We've got a job to do."

It was ten o'clock that evening when Mr. Sturgeon returned home to find his wife waiting for him anxiously.

"Well, William? What was so urgent that they had to contact you at this hour of the evening? Did it have anything to do with that awful yelling coming from the guest cottage after dinner?"

The Headmaster looked grim. "I have a theory about that, Mildred, but I don't think you're going to believe it."

"Why, whatever do you mean, dear?"

"Mildred, I have just witnessed the unclogging of no fewer than twenty-three toilets in our three dormitories."

Mrs. Sturgeon was taken aback. "Twenty-three in the same night?"

"Twenty-three in the same *hour*. And from each one we removed a glutinous mass of zucchini sticks, cemented in by sauce. I have rarely seen anything quite so disgusting."

"I don't think I understand."

"I devoutly wish *I* didn't. I took the liberty of checking the roster of Carson's football team. It matches exactly the map of plumbing disturbances at Macdonald Hall. Thank heaven a few of the players are roommates, or we would have had three more pipes to clear."

Light dawned on Mrs. Sturgeon. "The sounds from the cottage were a team meeting. Henry gave the boys zucchini sticks, and they — they disposed of them in the manner they felt best. How awful."

"It gets worse, Mildred. That tattling Blankenship boy told me that the idea for this assault on the plumbing came from Bruno Walton. . . ." He looked up at the ceiling. "Why didn't I know that?"

"Calm down, dear. It's all over now."

"On the contrary, Mildred — it hasn't even started yet. These twenty-seven boys are loyal to Carson not because of the football team, not because of the recreation hall they want, but because they somehow believe that overweight, muscle-headed ex-football player is 'one of the gang.' Why, while I was putting Walton and O'Neal on dishwashing duty for their evening's efforts, Walton was accepting it gladly, and begging me not to hold a grudge against Carson!"

His wife smiled sympathetically. "So it comes down to you against Henry, just like it was thirty years ago."

"I'm afraid not. This time it's me against everybody — Carson, the Board, and the students." He sighed heavily. "I'm getting too old for this."

3.
The
Zucchini
Disposal
Squad

Miss Scrimmage's sister was in town from Port Hope, and various girls had been selected to prepare for tonight's dinner party. Cathy Burton and Diane Grant were entrusted with baking the cake, an apple-crumb confection that was the Headmistress's favorite dessert.

Without much enthusiasm, Cathy sprinkled the final spoonful of brown sugar onto the crumb topping. "Okay, Diane. Fire up the oven. We're ready to roll."

Diane made no move. "Cathy, is there something wrong?"

"Why would you think something's wrong?" asked Cathy morosely.

"Because you mope twenty-four hours a day,"

replied Diane readily. "And you climb up to the roof every afternoon to watch Macdonald Hall practice football. And you do nothing but crab about how lousy they are. And now, for the very first time in your career as my roommate, you're about to serve Miss Scrimmage and her sister a *real* cake. No extra ingredients — no horseradish, no tabasco, no ground jalapeño peppers. Why, I'll bet you're not even planning to drop it on the floor. What's the matter with you?"

Cathy sighed. "I'm bored. All the excitement has gone out of school this year."

"It's only the second week," Diane pointed out.

Cathy nodded. "And by this time any other year, Bruno would be on some big crusade, and we'd be right up there with him."

"Risking our lives," Diane added feelingly.

"Having a *great time*," Cathy amended. "But this year, all they care about is football, which, as Bruno so kindly pointed out, is a *man's* game." Her face twisted. "We used to be part of what was going on at the Hall, Diane, and now we're left with this — baking a *crumb cake!*"

"I know the real reason for all this," Diane challenged. "You're jealous because they have a football team, and you used to love playing so much."

They were interrupted when Miss Scrimmage herself breezed in. "Now, let's see how our little dessert chefs are coming along." She dug a small spoon into the batter, tasted it, and paused thoughtfully. "Hmmm. Very nice. But it does lack that particular zing that you girls always put into your baking." Smiling, she whisked out of the kitchen.

30

"Okay," shrugged Cathy. "Break out the curry powder."

It was half an hour after lights-out, and eerie shadows played upon the walls of room 306 in Dormitory 3. Bruno and Boots, both holding flashlights in their dishpan hands, hunched over their desks, finishing their homework.

"This is your fault, you know," Boots said, not for the first time. "You were so busy thinking about Hank the Tank and football that you let The Fish sneak right up and zonk us from point-blank range."

"You know, it's beginning to get on my nerves, too," said Bruno thoughtfully. "I mean, twenty-some-odd toilets block, and only *we* get put on dishwashing duty."

"But we'll never be bored," said Boots with bitter sarcasm in his voice. "We've got classes till three-thirty, football practice till six, and we have to eat dinner, put in two hours of dishwashing, and finish all our homework by ten. It's a full life."

"It's only for a week," Bruno said soothingly. "We've got a bigger problem to deal with. What are we going to do the next time those zucchini sticks show up? I mean, Hank the Tank is a prince of a guy, but he's got a blind spot when it comes to that deep-fried soap he makes. We need a plan."

"I've already got a plan," Boots growled. "The next time somebody hands me a plate of zucchini sticks, I'm going to take it and throw it in the woods."

Bruno leaped to his feet. "That's a great idea! The woods behind the school! The Tank'll never go there! Boots, you're a genius!"

"I was joking! You can't throw stuff in the woods. That's pollution."

"It can't be," Bruno argued. "Nobody goes there. It's like the famous philosopher who said, 'If a zucchini stick falls in the forest and there's no one there to see it, does it make a mess?'"

"Hey, did you guys know that Mortimer Day is in love with the gym teacher at Scrimmage's?" blabbed Myron Blankenship at practice the next day.

"Shut up!" snapped Dave Jackson.

"He sends her love poems every day."

"Shut up!"

"They're really lousy."

"*Shut up!*"

"They don't even rhyme."

Bruno adjusted his helmet. "I think I just figured out how The Fish knew it was me who came up with the idea to flush the zucchini sticks. Ten to one it was the blabbermouth over there."

"Yeah," agreed Boots. "We've got to watch ourselves around that guy."

Calvin Fihzgart was standing on the sidelines, pawing the ground and snarling. In his hands he cradled the large beefsteak tomato he had saved from the dining hall at lunch and taken along to all his afternoon classes. Suddenly he thundered out into the middle of the field, let go a bloodcurdling scream, dropped the tomato to the ground, and hurled himself on it.

Pete Anderson was bug-eyed. "What the heck was that for?"

"This was a little demonstration of what The Beast

is going to do to the other teams when we start playing games!" He got to his feet and carelessly brushed off the front of his jersey, which was oozing red tomato pulp.

Under the direction of Coach Flynn and Henry Carson, the boys began to work at the various drills designed to put them in condition and sharpen their skills. Mr. Carson had even bought a tackling dummy and weight-lifting equipment to make for a complete football workout.

Carson threw his hat to the ground in disgust. "He's down again!" he complained as Sidney Rampulsky took another spectacular spill trying to run through a double line of large truck tires. "He can catch a pass, he can run like a gazelle, but he can't stand on his own two feet!"

"I wouldn't know anything about that," said Coach Flynn coldly. "It's *your* team. I'm not even important enough to be invited to the team meeting."

Carson flushed. "Aw, Alex, I told you a hundred times — I just forgot. Honest. I'm just the assistant and the sponsor. This is your team."

The two watched as quarterback Boots O'Neal heaved a wobbly pass ten feet over the head of Larry Wilson and into the third row of bleachers.

"Mine, eh? I'm not sure I want them. Look, Hank, these are good kids, and they'll give a hundred percent, but you must have noticed that we've got very little talent out there. And a couple of real nuts, too. Did you catch that act with the tomato?"

"They can learn," said Carson absently, watching the tackling dummy take out Wilbur Hackenschleimer. "You can't judge the talent until they get a feel for the game."

After the warm-up, Flynn lined the offensive team up against the defensive team for a short scrimmage.

"Come on, Calvin," called Boots. "Hurry up. We're getting ready to start."

Calvin joined them, his voice raspy from growling. "I don't understand why no one's calling me The Beast."

"Hey, Beast, you're facing the wrong way," piped Larry.

Finally they got Calvin into the right lineup, and the scrimmage began, with Boots directing the offensive team slowly down the field, more or less like a real football game.

"Okay," called Flynn. "Send in the punter."

Myron jogged onto the field.

Dave Jackson ran up to the coach, arms flung wide. *"Punter?* Why are we kicking? It's only third down!"

"Canadian rules, Jackson. You get three downs, not four. Remember?"

The Buffalo native looked crestfallen. "Three downs?"

The coach shrugged, almost apologetically. "Canadian rules."

Mortified, Dave slunk back to the huddle. "Man, I had strategy planned for that third down! I was going to run right, cut left, wiggle, dipsy-doodle, and finesse my way through for the TD. What a drag!"

"We're back, Elm," Bruno called, opening the door of room 201 and inviting himself and Boots in.

They were on their way home from dishwashing, and Bruno had insisted they stop by to get Elmer's plan for the rec hall.

Instantly the four Manchurian bush hamsters darted over to them and swarmed around their feet.

Elmer stepped away from his chemistry laboratory. "They're excited by the smell of dishwashing suds on your hands."

A distant siren was heard as a police car roared by Macdonald Hall on the highway. Suddenly the bush hamsters were out of control. Fur standing on end, they began bouncing up and down, grabbing at the two boys' legs, uttering sharp, high-pitched, chattering cries.

"Call off your monsters!" called Bruno, stumbling backward.

Boots grabbed onto him for support. "Help!"

The siren faded as the police car passed, and the animals quieted instantly.

"They always do that when they hear sirens," said Elmer calmly. "The frequency bothers their ears. You needn't have been frightened."

Boots took a couple of giant steps away from the four animals. "I don't know if I want them to reproduce," he said faintly. "Four is plenty."

"There's no worry about that right now," said Elmer, obviously depressed. "My tests are still negative."

"Bummer," said Bruno sympathetically. He spied a sheet of paper lying on top of the oscilloscope. "Hey, is this the rec hall? Great!" He examined the drawing with interest. "Elm, why are these tables so long? Wouldn't it be better to have small cafe-style tables?"

Elmer shook his head. "There'd be nowhere to run the gas lines for the Bunsen burners."

"*Bunsen burners?*" chorused Bruno and Boots in dismay.

"Of course," said Elmer, really warming to the discussion of his drawing. "What if you're in the recreation hall and you suddenly want to perform an experiment? Now, the ceiling is domed here for the planetarium — I have a sizable collection of prerecorded star lectures; but the dome is retractable, so the telescopes can be pointed at the sky. Now, in this corner I think we can fit two or three good-sized argon-neon lasers. And over here — "

"No, no, Elmer," Bruno interrupted. "Don't overwhelm us now. Thanks for the help. We'll get back to you."

As soon as they were out of the room, Boots burst out laughing. " 'Let's go to the smartest guy in the whole school,' " he mimicked. "Did you see that plan? The only thing missing was an embalming room for the guys who die of boredom!"

"Obviously, picking Elmer was a bit of a mistake," Bruno admitted. "We'll get someone else, that's all."

"Mildred," said Mr. Sturgeon upon returning home that afternoon, "the Ontario Ministry of Education has sent a curriculum inspector to make sure that we're up to scratch here at Macdonald Hall."

His wife smiled. "William, you know our teachers are among the best in the province, and our boys graduate with high standing. We have nothing to hide from this inspector."

The Headmaster sat down heavily in his favorite

chair. "Any other year, Mildred, I'd agree with you. But this 'football fever' is unbecoming in an institution like Macdonald Hall. After decades of excellence, why must they come to check up on us the year we are afflicted with football and zucchini sticks?"

"Oh, dear, I see what you mean," she said. "Well, do you think the inspector will understand this? What's he like?"

The Headmaster grimaced. "He has a long pointy nose, which he is about to stick into my business. If he knows how to smile, he has not demonstrated this talent to me. And he intends to interview my instructors, sit in on my classes, and in general, make a complete nuisance of himself."

Mrs. Sturgeon smiled smugly. "Never mind, William. The man is probably just shy. I know the perfect way to bring him out."

Kevin Klapper, curriculum inspector for the Ministry of Education, resembled a five-foot ten-inch mosquito, painfully thin and round-shouldered, with insectlike beady eyes, and a long pointed nose. He sat stoically at the Headmaster's dining-room table, dwarfed by another guest, Henry Carson. Across the table sat Miss Scrimmage, cowering in terror at the nearness of a Ministry inspector.

Mrs. Sturgeon was just pouring the coffee. "So, Mr. Klapper, how is it that the Ministry came to choose Macdonald Hall? We were evaluated five years ago and found to be number one in the province."

Miss Scrimmage sank into her chair. Her school had recently ranked two hundred and seventeenth, and she had been praying that the subject would not come up.

Klapper dabbed delicately at his thin lips with a napkin. "According to the new rules, chapter 6, paragraph 32/1, subsection 4, all private schools are subject to random inspection by the Ministry."

"How nice," said Mr. Sturgeon flatly. His wife's dinner parties drove him mad.

"Well, you sure came at the right time," Henry Carson informed Klapper. "We're revving up the football team for a big season. Maybe you can catch a couple of games."

Klapper looked highly offended. "I do not approve of football," he said icily. "It is a destructive influence on men's lives."

"What are you talking about?" bawled Carson, squeezing the delicate china cup in his hamlike fist. "Football builds character! It builds *men!*"

"It builds slobs," replied Klapper primly.

Henry Carson was livid. "What makes *you* the big expert?" he challenged Klapper.

Klapper looked vaguely shamed. "I may not look it," he confessed, "but I was once a football addict. It filled my every waking moment. I spent my time in front of the television; I spent my money traveling all over the continent to games." He shuddered. "I lost my job! My wife left me! I didn't even notice! It was Super Bowl Sunday. . . ." He lapsed into sudden silence.

"Oh, you poor man!" sniffled Miss Scrimmage.

"We're back together again," Klapper went on, "and I got a new job. But it was because I swore off football forever."

In the silence that followed, everyone heard Mr. Sturgeon sigh with resignation.

"Would anyone care for some banana cream pie?" asked Mrs. Sturgeon brightly.

Bruno Walton didn't normally get up for breakfast. But on Friday morning before the monthly assembly, he was established at the end of a long dining-hall table, holding court.

"Okay, guys, here's our strategy for the assembly."

"Bruno, you don't need strategy for an assembly," Boots explained patiently. "You go, and then when it's over, you leave."

"But," Bruno reminded him, "at the end of *our* assemblies, you hear bells. And before you know it, you're looking at a plate of zucchini sticks."

"Good point," said Wilbur, digging into a mountain of French toast. "Lay the strategy on us."

"It's very simple. When the wagons come in, we act thrilled. Oh, wow, zucchini sticks. We line up, we get our plates, and we get out of there. We take them back and hide them in our rooms. And then, after lights-out, the Zucchini Disposal Squad visits every room, bags up the zucchini sticks, and throws them in the woods."

"Sounds good," said Pete. "Who's the Zucchini Disposal Squad?"

"Us," Bruno announced grandly. "We're the Zucchini Disposal Squad."

"Count me out," chorused several voices. Other boys just glared.

"Might I point out," said Elmer timidly, "that

what you're describing is against the rules."

"And we're supposed to be in training," Boots added. "What if Hank the Tank spot-checks our rooms and tracks us down, dumping a truckload of his precious zucchini sticks in the woods?"

A babble of protest rose.

"Well, that's fine," said Bruno. "Anybody who wants out, just leave your name and room number with Boots. The Squad won't bother you. You can get rid of your zucchini sticks yourself. You might even want to eat them."

"Bruno doesn't fight fair," said Sidney, pointing an accusing finger.

"He's a sleazeball," Wilbur agreed. "But this time he's right."

"Of course I'm right," said Bruno. "So spread the word. I want every single guy in on this."

"I think I can help with that," said Dave Jackson with a wry smile. "I've got this roommate — the Blabbermouth. You tell him a secret at five-thirty, and you can watch it on the six o'clock news!"

The strategy went without a hitch. Mr. Sturgeon began the assembly with his usual "study hard" lecture, and then turned the proceedings over to Henry Carson, who led a pep rally for the football team. This brought on baleful looks from Kevin Klapper. The zucchini wagons came right on schedule, and all seven hundred-plus students followed Bruno's instructions exactly. Bruno described it as "a thing of beauty."

After lights-out that night, the Zucchini Disposal Squad, at a hundred-percent attendance, began prowling the bushes from window to window, dumping plates of zucchini sticks and small containers of sauce into large green garbage bags.

It took three boys, each making several trips, to drag the twelve overstuffed bags across the north lawn, past the football stadium, and into the woods. The entire operation took less than an hour.

4.
The
Greenhouse
Effect

"*Peee-yew!*" exclaimed Coach Flynn at football practice the next afternoon. "The whole field smells like a garbage dump! What happened here?"

Bruno and Boots exchanged agonized glances. To them, as to most of the team, the stench was easily identifiable — rotting zucchini. Something had gone wrong with the perfect plan.

Larry jogged over to them. "Bruno, remember last night when Elmer said if we left the zucchini sticks in the bags, the plastic would create a greenhouse effect and the zucchini would rot, and you said 'Shut up, Elmer'?" He wrinkled his nose. "Well, I think I smell a greenhouse effect."

Boots went pale. "The Fish is going to go in there to check out the stink, and when he sees what it is, we'll get expelled! Or, worse, we'll have to clean it up!"

Fortunately Mr. Carson was off working with the defense, and Coach Flynn was fully occupied trying to keep Calvin Fihzgart from dismembering the tackling dummy. So Bruno and Boots had no trouble sneaking away from the field and sprinting undetected into the woods.

The smell was so strong the boys had to hold their noses as they ran to the scene of last night's stash. There an incredible sight met their eyes. At least twenty fat raccoons were rooting around in the remains of the torn garbage bags, gnawing the batter coating off the zucchini sticks. The heap had also attracted every fly in the county, and the swarm hung in the air like a black cloud.

"Oh, Bruno!" came Boots's smothered voice from behind his hand. "*What* are we going to do about this?"

Uncharacteristically Bruno had no answer. "Maybe we can just leave it, and act twice as amazed as everyone else when they find it."

"Why didn't you listen to Elmer?" Boots accused. "He knew this would happen!"

"Let's be fair. He didn't mention a word about raccoons."

"Bruno, you're joking, and I'm dying! If we can't get rid of this mess, The Fish is going to kill us!"

Bruno shrugged. "So we'll come back tonight and bury it."

"*Bury it!* The terrain in these woods is seventy-five percent rocks! You'd need dynamite to dig in here!"

Bruno kicked at the ground experimentally.

"Hmmm. I see what you mean. Well, where's a good burying place around here?"

"Let's pray The Fish doesn't know of one," said Boots feelingly, "or we'll be in it!"

Bruno snapped his fingers. "Scrimmage's apple orchard. It's perfect."

"You'll *never* convince the guys to do it," said Boots positively.

"Of course they'll do it. It's the only way."

Just after midnight, the Zucchini Disposal Squad marched into the woods, armed with shovels and more green garbage bags.

"To think that I could be safe and sound at Jefferson Junior High right now," Dave Jackson was muttering. "But no. I had to come to Canada so I could shovel up rotten zucchini sticks. Oh, that smell!"

"Bruno," grumbled big Wilbur, "I just want you to know that tonight is the end. You'll get no more loyalty from me after this. No human being should have to do what we're going to be doing."

"I don't see why *I* have to be here," whined Elmer. "If you'd listened to me last night — "

"Will you guys back off?" snapped Bruno, adjusting a high-powered flashlight. "I've got a nose, too, you know. This isn't my idea of a good time, so I don't want to hear any more complaining tonight."

"How about tomorrow?" asked Larry innocently.

"Hey, did you guys know that Perry Elbert cuts his toenails with a seven-inch bowie knife?" came the voice of Myron Blankenship.

Bruno stopped in his tracks. "Wait a minute —

44

who brought the Blabbermouth along?"

"Me," mumbled Dave. "It was either that or two weeks of 'Hey, did you guys know my roommate sneaks out in the middle of the night?' "

"Okay," said Bruno, "but you tell the Blabbermouth that if word of this gets out, he's going down in the pit with the zucchini."

"Hey," said Myron, "your secret is safe with me."

Boots shone his own flashlight to illuminate the zucchini mound. "There it is," he announced grimly. "Those things up above it are flies."

"Oh, wow!" gasped Mark Davies. "All in favor of making Bruno do it himself say aye."

There was a chorus of strangled ayes. But eventually the group set themselves to the distasteful task of shoveling the decayed zucchini into their bags.

The flies were terrible, and the workers battled against the smell by breathing as little as possible. Sidney succeeded in holding his breath so well that he blacked out, and toppled face first into the slop heap. Mark, his roommate, hauled him out.

"Sidney! Sidney, speak to me!"

"Where am I?" Sidney asked groggily. "And what's that terrible smell?"

They worked on, fueled by their desire to have it over with. But when the last bag was sealed, and they began dragging their load towards the highway, the smell came with them on the person of Sidney Rampulsky.

"It was an accident," said Sidney defensively.

"Come on, guys," said Boots. "Speed it up. We've got a lot of digging to do."

Grumbling all the way, the Disposal Squad

pulled, pushed, rolled, and carried its rancid cargo past the football stadium and the dormitories, and across the highway. They had quite a struggle heaving the bulky bags over the wrought-iron fence that surrounded Miss Scrimmage's Finishing School for Young Ladies. Finally they trooped into the orchard, almost exhausted. The first shift of diggers manned the shovels.

"Boo!!"

Boots jumped like a terrified rabbit. "Bruno — "

"Hi, guys." Cathy strolled onto the scene, a nervous Diane in tow. "What's going on?" She spied Elmer. "Oh, I get it. It's a Drimsdale experiment." She marched up to Elmer and shook his hand heartily. "Congratulations. You've created the ultimate stink bomb."

Elmer's throat closed up as it always did in the presence of girls.

Diane wrinkled her nose painfully. "What *is* it?"

Wilbur supplied the answer. "Rotting zucchini. Tons of it." He held out his shovel to Bruno. "It's your turn. Start digging."

At last the hole was deemed deep enough, and the green bags were dumped into it. When the earth was filled in, the only remnant of the smell was Sidney, and even he was beginning to fade.

Boots breathed a sigh of relief. "It's over!"

There was a sudden rustling in the underbrush behind them. Everyone wheeled just in time to see Miss Scrimmage burst onto the scene, dressing gown flapping, curlers bobbing, brandishing her shotgun.

"Halt!"

* * *

Henry Carson stepped out of Dormitory 3 and paused, a thoughtful expression on his face. Walton and O'Neal weren't in their beds, either. That made eight team members breaking training. Well, this was nothing unusual. Football players never obeyed the curfew. It was a tradition. Now, where would they be? His mind took him back thirty years to his own days at Macdonald Hall. Where would *he* be? Instantly he cast his eyes across the highway to Miss Scrimmage's Finishing School for Young Ladies. Sure. Where else?

He broke into a jog, crossed the highway at a trot, and leaped over the fence in a single bound. The orchard. There were voices in the orchard. He cut his pace and moved stealthily towards the sounds. There, in a small clearing, a horrible sight met his eyes. Miss Scrimmage was holding a group of boys at gunpoint. And most of them were football players!

"My team!" Hank the Tank Carson took off like a thundering buffalo. Roaring into the clearing, he left his feet and sailed through the air, hitting Miss Scrimmage just below the knees. The Headmistress went down like a sack of oats. She and Carson hit the ground with a resounding crunch.

Boom! Boom! Both barrels of the shotgun went off harmlessly into the air. Echoes of the blasts reverberated about the countryside.

"What a tackle!" breathed Cathy in awe.

Miss Scrimmage scrambled to her feet. *"Assault!"* she shrieked. With a wild swing, she brought the butt of the shotgun down on Henry Carson's head.

"Mr. Carson!" cried Bruno. He rushed over to the fallen zucchini tycoon. "Can you hear me? It's Bruno!" But the ex-linebacker was out cold.

47

By this time, the orchard was teeming with girls in pink nighties as Miss Scrimmage's dormitories emptied. There were lights on at Macdonald Hall as well, and pajama-clad boys were beginning to dot the campus, curious as to the source of the shotgun blasts. The more adventurous of them ran across the highway to witness the goings-on firsthand.

Through the milling crowd rushed a familiar figure in a red silk bathrobe and bedroom slippers. Mr. Sturgeon took in the scene in one horrified instant. He turned burning eyes on Miss Scrimmage.

"Woman, what have you done?"

"She didn't shoot anybody!" Diane blurted out. "She just hit him!"

Carson stirred and tried to sit up. "Ooooh!" he moaned, holding his head gingerly. "Did somebody get the license number of that truck?"

"See?" Cathy said triumphantly. "He's alive!"

Mr. Sturgeon looked around. Boys and girls were everywhere, but it was easy to locate the guilty parties. They were the sweaty, smelly ones not in pajamas. In some annoyance, he noticed that Kevin Klapper was there, wrapped in a gray dressing gown, leaning against a tree, making extensive notes on a small steno pad.

Boots grabbed Bruno. "The Fish is looking right at us!"

"Listen," said Bruno soothingly, "there are ten of us. Sure, we'll get nailed, but no more than the other guys."

The two watched in paralyzing horror as Myron Blankenship ran over to the Headmaster and began a long story, complete with gestures which left no doubt that he was describing every single action of the Zucchini Disposal Squad. He finished with his finger pointing directly at Bruno and Boots.

"That Blabbermouth!" Boots exclaimed. "I'll kill him!"

"No, you won't," said Bruno through clenched teeth. "*I'll* kill him!"

Finally Mr. Sturgeon and a few members of the Macdonald Hall staff managed to gather up the boys and Henry Carson and herd them back to their own side of the highway. Before sending them off to their rooms, a red-faced Headmaster directed the ten culprits to be in his office at eight o'clock in the morning.

"We're doomed!" Boots predicted mournfully.

"Come on, Sidney," said Mark kindly. "Let's get you into the shower."

Dave was trudging along ahead of the rest. "Three downs, and now this," he muttered, shaking his head. "You Canadians are nuts!"

Henry Carson, his head sporting a large white bandage, hefted his rake and regarded his neat mound of leaves.

"So I said, 'Mr. Sturgeon, if you're going to punish my players, you'll have to punish me, too.' And he put me on leaf-raking duty."

The Zucchini Disposal Squad was spread out all over the rolling lawns of Macdonald Hall, raking the mid-September leaves as part of their punishment for the previous night's incident. There was also a lot of dishwashing, essay writing, and suspension of privileges divided up among the squad's ten members.

"Come on, Mr. Carson," grinned Bruno, working his own section of grass. "You know you don't have to do this."

"Forget it," said Carson stoutly. "I refuse to allow The Fish to call my bluff. I'm holding out until he takes us *all* off punishment."

Boots laughed mirthlessly. "You'll wait a long time."

"Probably. It's unbelievable. Thirty years go by, and he still has my number. I'm in shock! My head hurts, too," he added, touching his bandage gingerly.

Bruno scanned the skies. "One of these days it'll rain, and we can get good and soaked, and sneeze in front of Mrs. Sturgeon. Then she'll shame The Fish into letting us off the hook."

Carson looked at him with a new respect. "I never thought of that. Well, we've got to look at The Fish's point of view, too. You know that needle-nosed guy who was at the riot last night? He's an inspector from the Ministry of Education."

"Oh, no," moaned Boots. "We really made a great impression."

Bruno shrugged. "It's not our fault Miss Scrimmage is crazy. But it does explain why The Fish got so steamed over a minor incident. I've never seen so many guys getting chewed out at the same time that they wouldn't all fit on the bench!"

Boots snorted. "It was memorable — all of us crammed in there like sardines, The Fish hitting the ceiling, Elmer whimpering, the Blabbermouth filling in extra details — "

"Come on, men," interrupted Mr. Carson, quickening his pace. "We've got to get all this done by football practice."

As Mr. Carson raked his way north towards the stadium, Bruno and Boots worked in the opposite direction, and soon found themselves alongside Myron and Dave, with Elmer Drimsdale not too far away.

Elmer looked at Bruno reproachfully. "I shouldn't be here, you know. I should be with my bush hamsters. Time could run out on the whole species while I'm raking leaves."

But Bruno's attention was on someone else. "Hey, Blabbermouth. How come you're so quiet today? All talked out? Ever eat a rake? Want to try mine?"

"Sorry about that," said Myron blithely. "It just slipped out."

"Slipped out?!" howled Boots. "Two hours of details just *slipped out*?"

Myron shrugged. "It won't happen again. Hey, you guys don't know about Chris Talbot's ingrown toenail."

"Shut up," said Dave.

"They're going to have to operate."

Dave looked earnestly at Bruno and Boots. "You see? Don't be too hard on him. He can't help it. He's a blabbaholic. Whatever goes in his ears comes out his mouth."

"Well, okay," said Bruno, "but from now on it's your responsibility to control the Blabbermouth. If he sells us out and we have to kill him, it's on your head."

Working together, the five boys were the last to finish, coming to stand exhausted in the shadow of an enormous mountain of leaves right in the center of the lawn behind the Faculty Building.

"I can't believe that after all this work we have football practice," gasped Boots. "I'd give anything for a shower and a nap."

Bruno shook his head. "Look." He pointed in the direction of the dormitories. "Here comes one of the guys already suited up."

Elmer frowned. "He's coming awfully fast."

Boots, who had the sharpest vision, suddenly went white. "It's The Beast!"

"Hey, Calvin," called Bruno. "What's your hurry? Come on — slow down. Hey, Calvin! Calvin — *hit the deck!*" The five boys dove out of the way as Calvin Fihzgart, roaring like a freight train, tucked the football into his chest, put his head down, and barreled full speed into the neatly piled leaves. So intense was his concentration that he didn't even hear the five cries of agony echoing through the blizzard of leaves in his wake.

Boots watched his receding back before picking up the rake and setting to the task of rebuilding the mound.

Twenty feet away stood Kevin Klapper, taking notes and looking on disapprovingly.

"Hah!" laughed Cathy, peering through her binoculars. "He bobbled that pass like it was a hot potato! Of course, it wasn't much of a pass. Boots may as well be throwing sofa cushions!"

She and Diane were in their usual perch atop Miss Scrimmage's roof, watching the Macdonald Hall football practice.

"Cathy, what's wrong with you? You haven't

stopped laughing all day. I thought you said this was a boring year."

Cathy was positively glowing. "Last night Hank the Tank Carson of the Green Bay Packers blindsided our little old Miss Scrimmage. And not only did she live through it, but she got up and knocked him silly! I've never been this proud in my life!"

"So the school year is saved," said Diane.

"Are you kidding?" chortled Cathy. "There are great days ahead! I was off track for a while, but Miss Scrimmage showed me the way."

"Cathy, you're making me nervous. What are you talking about?"

"The Macdonald Hall Warriors are hopeless. They need help. So tomorrow I'm joining the team."

Diane leaned forward. "It's really windy up here, Cathy. It sounded like you just said you're joining the team."

Cathy laughed again. "They need a quarterback — *I'm* a quarterback."

Diane looked horrified. "But it's a boys' team! They'll never let you play!"

"I don't intend to ask. We'll see about this 'man's game.' "

"But Cathy, this is crazy!"

"Shhh, Diane." She was at the binoculars once more. "I'm scouting my future teammates."

5.
Quarterback Sneak

Boots O'Neal, carrying his math books in one hand and his large gym bag in the other, jogged out the rear entrance of the Faculty Building, heading for the football stadium. He was going to be late for practice again. Mr. Stratton was a stickler for the schedule, but today had been even worse, because Kevin Klapper, the curriculum inspector, had sat in on the class.

"Pssst! Boots!"

Boots stopped short and looked around. There, hiding in a clump of bushes, was Diane Grant, beckoning madly.

"I can't stop, Diane. I'm late."

"But it's urgent! It's — it's a matter of life and death!"

Boots put down books and bag and ran over to the bushes. "What's wrong?"

"I can't tell you."

"What do you mean you can't tell me?"

"You're standing in broad daylight," she explained, "where just anyone can see you. If they come over to you, they'll find me. Come into the bushes."

In exasperation, Boots ducked behind a branch and entered the thicket. "Okay, make it fast."

"Do you promise not to tell anyone?"

"Cross my heart and hope to die!"

His line of sight obscured by a large juniper bush, Boots failed to see Cathy Burton dart from cover, nab his gym bag, and sprint off towards the stadium.

"You're late, O'Neal!" barked Coach Flynn. "We're starting with a scrimmage. Get over there."

Without speaking, Cathy, dressed in Boots's equipment and uniform, jogged over and found her place in the lineup. The ball was snapped to her, and she faded back as the receivers began to run their patterns, trying to elude the defense. Suddenly she reared back and fired a bullet pass through a sea of bodies. It struck the receiver, Sidney, full in the chest, knocking the wind out of him. The force of the ball was so strong that, clutching it, he staggered backward and fell over across the goal line.

Henry Carson's jaw dropped. "Did you see that?" he howled at Flynn. "What a throw! Attaway, O'Neal!"

Bruno ran over to the quarterback and awarded the shoulder pads a hearty punch. "Hey, Boots, where did you learn to pass like that?"

Cathy gave him her sweetest smile. "Hi, Bruno."

Bruno gawked. His mouth opened and closed several times, but no sound came out.

"Nice day for a football game, eh?"

"C-C-C-C-Cathy — ?" Bruno began.

But Cathy just turned around and jogged back to where Coach Flynn was setting up the next play. Bruno watched her receding back. The jersey read O'NEAL.

"Come on, Walton!" barked Flynn. "Move it! We're going to start from the 20 and see if we can work our way downfield."

It took exactly one play. After the snap, Cathy caught sight of Dave Jackson, open deep. She stepped deftly around a charging lineman, cocked her arm back, and let go the long bomb. The ball soared, a perfect spiral, and dropped neatly into Dave's outstretched hands.

Henry Carson was on his feet, loping across the field. "You're fantastic!" he bawled. "But you're not O'Neal! Who are you?"

Bruno stepped in front of Cathy. "You're right! This isn't O'Neal! He's — uh — someone — a guy — this is him."

"He's someone, all right!" Carson enthused. "A natural passer. What's your name, son?"

Bruno was babbling. "It's — a student! Yeah, that's it. A student. Someone who missed the tryouts but still wants to play. It's — "

"Elmer Drimsdale," supplied Cathy, distorting her voice with a hand to her mouth.

"Elmer Drimsdale!" repeated Bruno trium-

phantly. He staggered back and stared at her. *"El-mer Drimsdale?!"*

"Elmer Drimsdale?" chorused most of the players.

Flynn was thunderstruck. "Drimsdale? The genius? You play football?"

Cathy shrugged modestly.

"All right, Drimsdale," said Carson, "let's see what you can do."

Boots looked around the campus. Had everybody gone crazy? Not only had Diane run off on him, but his gym bag was missing. He was fifteen minutes late for practice, with no uniform, no equipment, and no idea what was going on.

He headed off in the direction of the stadium, arriving just in time to see his uniform throw a beautiful touchdown pass.

"Hey, O'Neal," called the coach. "I'm moving you to the offensive line. Drimsdale's taking over at quarterback."

Boots just stared.

Bruno jogged over. "Act like it makes sense. I'll explain later."

"You mean our new quarterback is *Cathy?*" exclaimed Boots in disbelief at dinner that night.

"Shhh! Yes!" said Bruno. "But if someone asks, it's Elmer. Don't tell anybody else, and especially not the Blabbermouth!"

Wilbur sucked in a long string of spaghetti. "This is bad news," he pronounced darkly. "Cathy Burton is the only person I know who's crazier than Bruno.

If she doesn't get us expelled, she'll land us in jail."

"Don't be an idiot," said Bruno. "She's *great.* She's going to get us our rec hall."

"I don't suppose you've considered," said Larry, "that if word of this got out, our team would probably be disqualified."

"Where is it written that girls can't play football?" said Bruno.

"Yeah, but she's not a Macdonald Hall student," Boots pointed out.

"There's always been a special relationship between the Hall and Scrimmage's," Bruno insisted. "Besides, she's our best player." He paused and beamed. "And now that we're back on the rec hall trail, we need a volunteer to draw up a good plan for the building."

"Hey, no problem," said Larry sarcastically. "I'm only a student, the office messenger, a football player, a dishwasher, a leaf raker, and the author of a twenty-five-hundred-word punishment essay for The Fish. I might as well be an architect, too."

"Yeah. Do it yourself," agreed Sidney.

"I'll do it," Wilbur volunteered from the depths of a Pudding Pop.

"You?" asked Mark. "I thought you said zucchini disposal night was the end."

"This is different," said Wilbur. "After all I've been through over this dumb rec hall, I'm not taking any chances that it'll come out lousy."

"Great," said Bruno. "I think that's every-thing — "

At that moment, Elmer Drimsdale hurried over to the table, his face haunted. "Bruno, I just had the strangest encounter. I met Mr. Carson in the hall, and he picked me up and lifted me high into the air, and congratulated me, and said I was the greatest little guy in the world. I told him he was premature, because my bush hamsters haven't mated yet. And then he laughed, and swung me around, and said he loved my sense of humor." Elmer looked around the table. His listeners were all doubled over with laughter.

"Now I know what I left out!" Bruno choked. "I forgot to tell Elmer!"

"Oh!" Elmer was incensed. "You think this is funny! It was terrifying! He had me way up in the air!"

Bruno motioned Elmer to a chair. "There are times when a man, for the good of his school, must go along with something that *may* seem a little weird. The fact is, Elm old pal, everyone thinks you're the star quarterback of the Macdonald Hall Warriors. You aren't — don't worry. But say you are just in case anybody asks."

"What kind of an explanation was that?" asked Boots in disgust. He turned to Elmer, who seemed dazed. "Look, Cathy from Scrimmage's is going to play for our team. We can't say it's her, so we have to say it's you. Got it?"

"But why me?" Elmer asked plaintively.

"Because Cathy told everybody she was you. So we're stuck with it."

Elmer thought it over. "Am I a good football player?"

"Hey," said Bruno, "you're the star of the team."

"Well, I guess in that case it's all right."

Myron Blankenship appeared, Dave a few paces behind him. "Hi, gang. What's new?"

"Nothing!" chorused everybody.

Larry pointed to the kitchen. "There's Hank the Tank reporting for dishwashing duty. I just can't believe he's going through this punishment with us. He's one in a million."

"Who's on with him tonight?" asked Dave.

"Boots and me," said Bruno, picking up his tray. "Come on. Let's go."

"All right!" bawled Coach Flynn at his twenty-seven players. "Who put the teeth marks on the tackling dummy?"

There was no answer, but twenty-six pairs of eyes turned to Calvin Fihzgart.

"It was The Beast!" Calvin growled proudly. "Just a little preview of what I'm going to do once the season starts!"

Flynn looked disgusted. "The object of the game is to *beat* the other team, not *eat* the other team. Behave yourself."

"Hey, I'm just getting pumped up."

Everyone was getting pumped up. Cathy Burton was the driving force, wearing number 00, with DRIMSDALE printed across the back. On her nose sat an old pair of Elmer's horn-rimmed glasses with the lenses popped out. Her long hair was pinned up under her helmet.

Coach Flynn's opinion was: "They're the same stumblebums they always were, but with Drimsdale at quarter, at least they're a team."

"There's plenty of time," said Henry Carson smugly. "You'll see."

"How is Cathy going to manage to sneak over here at three-thirty every single day?" Boots mused as he and Bruno watched her fire perfect pass after perfect pass for the receivers' drills.

Bruno laughed. "She told Miss Scrimmage that she's taking up bird-watching. She's supposed to be on the trail of the elusive kiki bird."

Bruno's main concern remained keeping Cathy's identity from Myron Blankenship. So far all was well. Myron was the team kicker, and was usually practicing away from the rest of the players. And each day, Cathy would leave the field a few minutes ahead of everyone else, which was easily explained. Football or no football, Elmer Drimsdale still had a lot of experiments to attend to.

Since the coming of "Drimsdale," interest in the Warriors had begun to spread beyond the players and their coaches. During the practices, the bleachers were sprinkled with spectators, and most of the boys were looking forward to cheering the team on this season. Elmer, who had to lie low during practice so as not to be seen in two places at once, was becoming an object of admiration.

Kevin Klapper, meanwhile, was hard at work updating the Macdonald Hall file for the Ministry of Education. He had not actually visited the football stadium, but he had certainly heard about the Macdonald Hall Warriors in many student conversations. To a reformed football addict, all the danger signs were there. Macdonald Hall was about to succumb to footballmania. That riot at the girls' school had been the first sign. It was no coincidence that eight of the ten culprits had been football players. Of course, Sturgeon assured him that no drop in grades would be tolerated, but this could not last.

Sure, it all seemed innocent now. He remembered himself in the early days of his own footballmania. First Sunday afternoon games, then cable television — college, even high school ball. Then the plane trips, rare at first, but growing more and more frequent. His concentration began to go after that. He would sit in the office mulling over last night's game in his mind, searching for holes in the defense, and hatching strategies. And then . . . Klapper shook himself. No, there was no way even the top-rated boarding school in Ontario could hold up against the ravages of this destructive game. By midseason, they'd be lucky if anyone even *cared* about getting a passing grade.

And Kevin Klapper would be there to expose it all, and prove that football would never get the better of him again.

"I'll bet Wilbur's come up with a great rec hall plan," said Bruno as he and Boots entered Dormitory 2. "He's a bit of a crab, but in the end, he's a pretty smart guy."

Boots stepped into the main hallway and stopped dead. There was a small crowd of boys standing around the open door of the room Wilbur shared with Larry Wilson. Laughter could be heard, and much heckling.

Bruno elbowed his way through the group and looked into the room. Wilbur stood in the center of the floor, bellowing with outrage. Larry had him in a full nelson to keep him from hurling himself upon Elmer Drimsdale, who cowered before him, clutching his four bush hamsters to his heart.

"Five pounds of imported halvah! *Gone!*" Wilbur

shouted in a foghorn voice that echoed throughout the dormitory.

"I'm sorry," said Elmer meekly. "They got out of my room, and I couldn't catch them. They're not responsible. Don't yell at them; yell at me."

"I *am* yelling at you! My cookies! Half my chips! The mixed nuts are *decimated!* They even got into the — the *peanut butter!*" He broke free from Larry and yelled the last part into Elmer's face. The bush hamsters scrambled, and buried their heads in Elmer's shirt.

Elmer drew himself up to his full height, which was a good eight inches shorter than Wilbur. "Wilbur Hackenschleimer, you ought to be ashamed of yourself! You're scaring my Manchurian bush hamsters, an endangered species! How do you expect them to reproduce when they're all distraught like this?"

"I don't care if they *never* reproduce!" roared Wilbur. "I want my peanut butter!"

"Hold everything!" Bruno rushed in between them. "Break it up. We're all friends here, remember? Wilbur, we'll get you some new food. Elmer, take your rats and go home."

Wilbur was not consoled. "Look what they ate!" He showed Bruno torn bags and gnawed boxes.

Even Bruno was impressed. "How long were they in here?"

"Only ten minutes," said Larry in awe. "Wilbur himself couldn't put away that much in ten minutes."

Bruno looked at Elmer. "Do they eat like this all the time?"

"Oh, yes," said Elmer. "Each bush hamster can

consume seven to ten times his own weight daily. And they'll eat practically anything."

Bruno raised both eyebrows. "Anything? Even if it's lousy?"

Elmer nodded.

Bruno emitted a great shout of triumph. "That's it! We've got four new recruits for the Zucchini Disposal Squad! The next time Hank the Tank gives us zucchini sticks, these little guys can eat them for us!"

"I can't see any harm in it," said Elmer thoughtfully.

Boots pushed his way through the crowd. "Just in case anybody's thinking of speaking his mind, the Blabbermouth's here."

Bruno dropped his voice to a whisper. "Don't tell the Blabbermouth about the new zucchini disposal plan. This is the solution we've been praying for." To Wilbur he said, "Have you got that layout for our rec hall finished yet?"

"Rec hall? *Rec hall?* How can you talk about a rec hall when my food — my life — my sustenance has been ransacked by a gang of mangy rodents?"

Elmer was outraged. "It is well known in the scientific community that Manchurian bush hamsters are extremely clean animals!"

Muttering darkly under his breath, Wilbur handed Bruno his rec hall drawing just as Myron Blankenship broke through the crowd.

"What's all the excitement?" Myron asked.

Bruno held up the floor plan. "We're all admiring this great drawing."

Myron looked confused. "Uh — very nice."

* * *

64

"Hey, did you guys know that Elmer Drimsdale keeps furry animals in his room?" announced Myron Blankenship in geography class the next day as the boys were settling into their seats.

Boots O'Neal turned beseeching eyes upward. "Is there no end to his yap?"

Bruno looked disgusted. "Poor Elmer. When his bush hamsters get booted out, he'll be heart-broken."

"So you think this is going to get back to The Fish or one of the teachers?" Boots asked.

Bruno nodded grimly. "It might be tomorrow, it might take a month, but the Blabbermouth always gets his man. And this doesn't do much for our zucchini disposal plan, either. We can't very well feed that stuff to the hamsters if they're not here. I've got half a mind to feed it to the Blabber-mouth."

Boots shook his head. "What a disaster last night was. The fight of the century, the bush hamsters got spotted by the Blabbermouth — and let's not forget Wilbur's rec hall plan."

"Don't remind me," Bruno groaned. "I thought that guy was smart. I forgot that his idea of recre-ation is a restaurant. Pizza ovens! Barbecue pits! Soda fountains! A salad bar! Why, there must have been six refrigerators in that drawing — seven if you include the meat locker!"

Boots snickered. "That's Wilbur. His head is ruled by his stomach."

"All right, laugh. Three floor plans, all of them useless. I'd like to see *you* put in some effort before you chuckle the house down."

"As a matter of fact, I will," said Boots. "I'll draw

the next plan, just to show you what a realistic rec hall should be like."

Mr. Klapper appeared in the doorway, notebook in hand. "Aha! Ninety seconds after start of the period, and this class is not yet underway." His eyes narrowed. "Are there any *football players* here?"

Mystified, Bruno, Boots, and Myron raised their hands. Klapper made notes.

Myron stood up. "Sir, did you know that Elmer Drimsdale keeps furry animals in his room?"

Klapper's thin eyebrows shot up. "Drimsdale. He's your new *quarterback*, isn't he?" He made even more notes, and left the room.

Three football players in a late class. The star quarterback keeping animals in his room. The case against Macdonald Hall was building.

"One more bench press," Bruno puffed, "and I'm going to drop dead before we ever play a game!"

It was six-thirty in the morning, and Bruno and Boots were in the Macdonald Hall gym, lifting weights.

"Cathy's life is in our hands," Boots grimaced, chinning himself on a high bar until his fair face turned purple. "I'll admit that she's a million times better than the rest of us put together, but she's still a girl, and this is a rough game. As offensive linemen, we're the only thing standing between her and the big guys on the other teams. We have to train our heads off!"

"Hold on a minute," said Bruno. "You can get me up in the middle of the night and put ten-thousand-pound barbells in my hands, but you can't pull the wool over my eyes. We didn't hold a gun to Cathy's head and force her to be our quarterback, remember? She stole your stuff and snuck out onto the field."

"Sure," said Boots. "But we also didn't jump right up and say, 'No, she can't play. She'll get killed. And she doesn't even go to Macdonald Hall.' "

So in the days leading up to the Zucchini Warriors' first game, as the team trained and practiced, Bruno and Boots trained and practiced more than anyone. And they prepared themselves mentally more than anyone, except Calvin Fihzgart. Calvin had worked himself up into such a state of ferocity that Coach Flynn had to threaten to bench him after an incident where he'd uprooted a small cedar shrub with his bare hands and hurled it across the highway.

"Look, Fihzgart, never mind the landscaping! Concentrate on playing football!"

"Coach, I'm just showing you what's going to happen. That tree is a player from the other team when he comes up against The Beast!"

The opening of the football season was a home game on Saturday afternoon, and Mr. Carson scheduled a team meeting at his cottage Thursday night. Naturally Elmer had to attend rather than Cathy, but Boots brought along a cassette recorder to tape the strategy session for the absent quarterback.

"Remember," Bruno whispered, "if Hank the Tank comes up with zucchini sticks, don't panic. Elmer's still got his bush hamsters, and they can take care of the whole shipment."

The boys arranged themselves in the living room, and Coach Flynn shut the door.

"Men," Henry Carson said dramatically, "we've come a long way, and Saturday is our first test."

67

All the players cheered. Even Elmer looked enthusiastic.

"The opponents we drew are the St. Vincent Junior High Voles, and they're not a very strong team. They finished in the cellar last year."

"And they're going to finish in the cemetery this year!" roared Calvin.

"Don't get overconfident," Flynn warned seriously. "Even though the Voles lost all their games last season, they can still be tough. Remember, this is only our first game. But we can still do our best and make a good showing — "

"Good showing?!" interrupted Mr. Carson. "We can beat those guys! But we have to play a tight defense and a careful offense. Right, Drimsdale?"

"Oh — uh — indubitably, sir," said Elmer.

"He means yeah," supplied Bruno.

"Right." Mr. Carson wheeled out a chalkboard. "Now we're going to go over all our plays. Drimsdale, front and center."

They went on for the better part of an hour, running the few plays that the Warriors had worked on in practice.

"So that's our 85 Buttonhook," said Coach Flynn after a long explanation. "Now, Drimsdale, why does it work?" .

Elmer examined the blackboard thoughtfully. "Because of the trigonometric ratios of the trajectory of the ball as it leaves the quarterback's hand, compensated with the downward acceleration of the gravitational pull of the earth?" he suggested.

Flynn stared at the board. "Maybe," he said finally. "But I was going to say that it works because the other guys are way down here."

68

the quarterback of the Macdonald Hall Warriors. "My first game! I've never been this excited in my life!"

"What was all that growling on the tape? Or was someone watching 'Valley of the Dinosaurs' in the next room?"

"Oh," said Cathy airily, "that was The Beast, one of our players. Cute little guy. Calvin Somebody."

Diane swallowed hard. "Cathy, I know how much you love football, and I know you're fantastic, but are you sure you want to go through with this?"

"Of course I'm sure! You think I've done all this work so I can *not* play?"

"But Cathy, this isn't practice where they know you're a girl! This is a whole other team just itching to knock somebody's brains out! And as the quarterback, you're target number one!"

Cathy made a face. "Look, Diane, you've been listening to Miss Scrimmage for so long that you've started believing all that stuff about how young ladies are delicate flowers that fall apart at the slightest touch. Sure, I might not be as strong as some of those guys, but the big ones are the slow ones, and with any luck, I can stay out of their way. Okay, the team isn't great, but we've been working like crazy. And linemen protect the quarterback, whether she's a girl or not."

Diane sat down on her bed, frowning. "I don't know. You've done some crazy things before, but tomorrow — I think about it, and I still can't believe it."

"Believe it," said Cathy. "Because tomorrow 'Elmer Drimsdale' is going out there to show them how it's done!"

"That makes sense, too," said Elmer generously.

"Okay," said Mr. Carson. "We'll have a light practice tomorrow — I want everybody to be at a hundred percent for Saturday."

"We won't let you and the coach down, Mr. Carson," said Bruno earnestly, "will we, guys?"

"*NO!!*" bellowed twenty-six voices.

"That's my team!" said Carson emotionally. "So grab some zucchini sticks, men, and have a good night."

The zucchini wagon was at the door, bells ringing.

Myron looked surprised. "But Mr. Carson, don't you know what we did with the last — ?"

Two hands clamped heavily over Myron's open mouth. Dave Jackson and Pete Anderson, one lifting under each arm, hoisted him up and carried him out of the house, pausing only to receive three plates of zucchini sticks at the door. Bruno flashed them the thumbs-up signal.

Mr. Sturgeon walked across the campus in the direction of the dormitories. He disliked what he was about to do, but do it he must. There was a rumor circulating that Elmer Drimsdale was harboring some sort of animal, and the rumor had reached the ears of Miss Hildegarde, the school nurse. That tattling Blankenship boy had no doubt started it all. And now the Headmaster was forced to finish it. Personally he had nothing against Elmer keeping animals for his scientific studies. But rules were rules, and Miss Hildegarde had been extremely adamant on the phone. Still, interfering with Drimsdale's experiments always seemed like a crime against science.

He entered Dormitory 2, approached the door of room 201, and knocked.

"It's not locked," came a voice that was definitely not Drimsdale's. "Step right up. Bring 'em all in. They're eating them faster than we can stuff them in the cage."

Mr. Sturgeon entered to see Bruno, Boots, and Elmer on their hands and knees around a large cage, feeding zucchini sticks to four furry gray-brown creatures.

Not looking away from the cage, Bruno stretched out his hand towards the newcomer. "Come on. Hand over your plate. We haven't got all night, you know."

"Good evening, Walton — O'Neal — Drimsdale."

All three scrambled to their feet.

"S-S-Sir," stammered Bruno. "What a surprise!"

"I see you've restaffed the Zucchini Disposal Squad," said the Headmaster with some amusement. "What on earth are they?"

"They're Manchurian bush hamsters, sir," said Elmer, "an endangered species. I'm attempting to make them reproduce."

The door burst open, and Larry and Wilbur entered. "Okay, we've got two more plates of garbage — Mr. Sturgeon — " Wilbur barely whispered. "Uh — we were just — uh — leaving, and — uh — good-bye." The two put down their plates and fled.

Mr. Sturgeon stared in amazement at the huge stack of empty Mr. Zucchini plates, and then at the four little bush hamsters in the cage. "Well, Drims-

dale, I'm afraid I have some bad news for you. Would you prefer that Walton and O'Neal leave us?"

"It's no problem, Elm," said Bruno. "We could come back later and you could tell us then."

"That won't be necessary," said Elmer bravely. He turned to the Headmaster. "This has something to do with my bush hamsters, sir?"

"I fear so, Drimsdale. And I tell you honestly that I hate to do this. I find it commendable that you wish to save this species from extinction. But too many people know about this already, and keeping animals in this room is very clearly against the rules. You will have to move them elsewhere." He glared down the wide smile of inspiration on Bruno's face. "No, Walton. This includes your room and anyone else's room. And it also includes the rooms of all of the young ladies across the road, since *we do not go there anymore*. Am I right?" This time it was the Headmaster's turn to smile. "Now, Drimsdale, you may have a day or so to try and find another home for your bush hamsters. But if you cannot, perhaps you had better return them to their owners."

"Yes, sir," said Elmer.

Cathy hit the eject button, and out popped her recording of the team meeting. It was Friday night before the big game. Earlier, she had retrieved the cassette from where Bruno and had hidden it in the Macdonald Hall bushes roadside.

"Well, do you know it yet?" asked Diane sarcastically. "You've only listened to it three

"We're as ready as we're ever going to

6.
Welcome to Macdonald Hill

Saturday was a perfect day for football, brisk but sunny. The game was scheduled for two, but many of the players were in the locker room by noon. Hank the Tank Carson was already there, pacing the length and breadth of the room, a bundle of nerves.

The bus carrying the St. Vincent Junior High Voles arrived an hour and a half before game time, and Calvin Fihzgart was on hand to evaluate their opponents as they filed into the visitors' locker room.

"Those poor guys," he said to Pete Anderson, genuine pity in his ferocious eyes. "They're totally doomed. They have to get on the field against the roughest, toughest, meanest guy in the whole league!"

"Who's that?" asked Pete absently. He was noting that the other players looked extremely large, and pretty confident for a last-place team.

"Who's that?!" Calvin growled in disbelief. "Me! The Beast! The one-man wrecking crew! The tower of evil! The baddest guy alive! The roughest, toughest — "

"Oh, right," said Pete. "I forgot."

Bruno, Boots, and Elmer entered the locker room carrying the Manchurian bush hamsters in their cage.

Mr. Carson was appalled. "Almost an hour to game time, and you're playing with kittens!"

"Elmer's under a lot of pressure to get these bush hamsters out of his room," Bruno explained.

"Pressure? What kind of an idiot leans on the star quarterback right before the big game?"

"Mr. Sturgeon," Bruno admitted.

Carson looked disgusted. "It figures."

"Do you think maybe they could live somewhere in the clubhouse?" Boots suggested. "There's a spare equipment room."

"Yeah, sure, anywhere!" said Carson impatiently. "I'll put them up at the Hilton if it'll take the heat off my quarterback! But hurry up! You should be dressing!"

Around one o'clock, the stands started to fill up with the staff and students of Macdonald Hall. Soon, though, Miss Scrimmage led her entire school over for "a delightful afternoon of sport," and there was a battle royal for the best seats. A number of local farm families, and a few townspeople from nearby communities were also on hand, and the mobile unit from CHUT-TV in Chutney was setting up to get a few action shots for the evening sportscast. The St. Vincent team had brought some supporters of their own.

Miss Scrimmage's cheerleading squad was warming up. Each of the nine girls wore a bright red uniform with THE LINE OF SCRIMMAGE spelled out in sequins on the back.

Mr. Sturgeon was leading his wife towards the stadium when an enormous eighteen-wheel tractor trailer backed up to the main entrance. The rear door folded down into a ramp, and out pedaled twenty-four Mr. Zucchini bicycle wagons, cabinets steaming, bells ringing.

"Oh, Lord!" groaned the Headmaster. "When the Zucchini Disposal Squad sees this, we won't have a football game; we'll have a cry-in!"

"Come on, William. Let's find our seats. Mercy, I'm excited!"

Mark Davies had been practicing all week, learning how to operate the stadium scoreboard for the game. As the spectators settled in, they were greeted by the message:

** WELCOME TO MACDONALD HILL **

Back in the locker room, all the players were suited up, present, and accounted for except one.

"*Where's Drimsdale?*" bellowed Coach Flynn in great agitation.

"Easy, Alex," said Mr. Carson, who was himself pacing the floor. "You know how eccentric he is.

75

He's probably dressing back at the dorm. He'll be here when we take the field."

As if on cue, Cathy poked her helmeted head into the dressing room, and waved. A great sigh was heaved.

The Voles were already warming up when the Macdonald Hall Warriors thundered out onto the field. The crowd broke into applause. Miss Scrimmage's girls, every single one of them aware of the true identity of number 00, went berserk, chanting *"El-mer! El-mer!"*

Mr. Sturgeon's brow furrowed. "Drimsdale appears to be acquiring something of a following," he commented.

His wife glowed. "Isn't that a wonderful surprise? Our top student is our top athlete."

The Headmaster frowned. "Wonderful," he agreed vaguely.

Calvin Fihzgart was looking around, scowling. "Hey! Where's the ambulance? I thought there was going to be an ambulance on hand!"

Sidney shrugged. "What for?"

"What do you mean 'what for?' The Beast is playing!"

Macdonald Hall won the coin toss and chose to receive the kickoff. The ball was caught by Dave Jackson, who tucked it away and took off, Wilbur and Calvin blocking ahead of him. They made it up to their own 40-yard line before being stopped by the Voles' defense. There was a small pileup, and the play was whistled dead.

Wilbur, Dave, and the three Voles got briskly to their feet, but there was still a Macdonald Hall jersey lying on the ground.

On the sidelines, Boots stood up. "It's The Beast! He's down!"

"How could he be down?" said Bruno. "Nothing happened!"

Mr. Carson and Coach Flynn rushed onto the field to attend to their injured player.

"Where's the stretcher?" roared Calvin, outraged.

"What's wrong?" asked the coach breathlessly. "He hardly even hit you!"

"My arm," said Calvin, cradling his right elbow. "I think it's a compound fracture."

They helped him over to the bench where Miss Hildegarde, the school nurse, examined his elbow. Calvin bore all this bravely. "It's a compound fracture, right?"

She stared at him. "It's just a bruise."

"The Beast would not get 'just a bruise,' " seethed Calvin. "With him it's either a compound fracture or nothing."

"Then it's nothing," she said coldly.

By this time, Mr. Sturgeon had left his seat and rushed to the bench. "Perhaps we had better take the boy for X rays."

As the Headmaster and the nurse left with Calvin, and the offensive team took the field, a very nervous Boots O'Neal sidled up to the quarterback.

"Cathy, if you want to take off out of here, I'll cover for you."

Behind Elmer's empty glasses, Cathy laughed. "You want to take off? I'll cover for *you*. I came to play."

"But Cathy, a guy got injured already!"

"Stow it, Melvin. We're lining up."

Nervously Boots took his place in the line beside Bruno. "Remember," he hissed to his roommate. "No one touches her — even if we have to die for it!"

From his pocket, Bruno produced his lucky piece, a penny set in the center of an imitation-silver four-leaf clover. He kissed it quickly and put it away.

As the ball was snapped, two big Voles came charging forward, trying to get to Cathy. "This is it!" Boots heard Bruno cry as the four met with a resounding crunch. The two Macdonald Hall Warriors stood firm, pushing against the attackers with all their might. Just as Bruno felt his strength almost gone, there was a whistle, and the two Voles trotted off. He looked around, dazed. Cathy had completed a pass to Dave Jackson for a Warriors' first down.

"Hey, wow," said Bruno, terribly pleased. "We protected the quarterback. We're great!"

Last place or not, the St. Vincent Voles were the better team, but Cathy Burton was unstoppable. Her passes were so perfect that the Macdonald Hall receivers could not possibly drop all of them. Cheered on by the enthusiastic Warrior fans and the half-demented girls from Miss Scrimmage's, she led the team down the field for the first touchdown of the game. The Voles struck back, and the Warriors' defense completely fell apart. Score tied, 7–7. The Voles added a field goal and, miraculously, Myron Blankenship succeeded in kicking the ball between the uprights to knot the score at 10 a few seconds before the end of the first quarter.

"Attaboy, Blankenship!" cheered Mr. Carson as

the players were jogging to the sidelines. "Nice kick!"

"Mr. Carson, did you know that Gary Potts has dandruff?" responded Myron, apparently untroubled by first-game jitters.

"Concentrate on the game," advised Coach Flynn.

The second quarter was all Cathy. She was brilliant, throwing for three touchdowns amid tumultuous chants of "El-mer, El-mer," in the stadium. Each time she completed a pass, the scoreboard read ** DRIPSDALE ** in her honor. By halftime, Macdonald Hall led 31–26.

Henry Carson and Coach Flynn were ecstatic. "We've got them!" Carson cried, dancing around the locker room in his excitement. "Drimsdale, you're incredible! Did you ever consider playing college ball?"

Smiling at Bruno and Boots, Cathy nodded enthusiastically.

At that moment, Miss Hildegarde and Calvin Fihzgart entered the room. Calvin's left arm was bandaged, and wrapped in an elaborate sling, bent at the elbow.

Coach Flynn gawked at the sling. "What was it?"

The nurse looked completely disgusted. "He has a slightly bruised elbow."

"So what's with the sling?" asked Mr. Carson.

"It's his pillowcase!" she snorted. "And the bandage is electrical tape!"

"It's going to hurt like crazy when I take it off, too!" said Calvin proudly. "Only The Beast could stand that kind of pain!"

Coach Flynn sighed. "Okay, Fihzgart. Why don't you sit out the rest of the game? We can talk later about whether you'll be ready to play again next week."

As Mr. Carson and Coach Flynn launched into a rousing halftime pep talk, Calvin found himself a seat in the stands among a large group of Miss Scrimmage's girls. Soon he was nicely settled in, explaining to an enraptured audience how The Beast had acquired his football injury.

The halftime show consisted of the Macdonald Hall band, and the Line of Scrimmage, who featured a special tribute to quarterback Elmer Drimsdale. The Mr. Zucchini vendors used the break in the action to pass out more free zucchini sticks. Some of these found their way into the stomachs of the spectators, but the vast majority were nonchalantly thrown under the bleachers.

Great cheering welcomed the Warriors as they stampeded onto the field for the second half. The scoreboard read ** NO TEAM **.

Bruno slapped his forehead. "That's supposed to be *Go* Team!" he bellowed up at where Mark sat, but his voice was lost in the roar of the audience.

From the very beginning of the third quarter, it was obvious that the Voles had taken on new life. Almost immediately they thundered down the field to take the lead with a touchdown. When Cathy came on to direct Macdonald Hall's counterattack, the Warriors were smothered by the Voles' defense. Before the quarter was up, the Voles had added another field goal, to make the score 36–31 against the home team.

"Don't panic!" panicked Coach Flynn during a time-out. "We can win this game, but we have to keep cool."

"It's all up to you, Drimsdale," Henry Carson added, putting a hand on Cathy's shoulder. "Now's your chance to show what kind of man you are!"

Kevin Klapper stepped out of the Macdonald Hall spare cottage into the brisk September air. He had not felt this refreshed and uplifted in years. Not five minutes earlier, he had finished his report, condemning Macdonald Hall for footballmania. He held the eleven typewritten sheets in his hands, skimming here and there. Oh, yes, they would feel the shock waves of this report inside the ivy-covered walls of Macdonald Hall.

He began to walk, the cool air invigorating him all the more. This was it! With this report he was putting his football obsession to rest forever. He was free.

A distant sound reached him, and he paused. It was hundreds, maybe thousands, of voices, cheering, rooting, and screaming together in one uninterrupted roar. It was coming from the football stadium, of course. Today was the first scheduled game for the Macdonald Hall Warriors. He looked at his report and shook his head sadly.

Still, it wouldn't hurt to have a look at the team that was putting a permanent blot on the spotless record of Macdonald Hall. His report under his arm, he headed across the campus to the north lawn. He walked into the stadium, and peered downfield critically.

Macdonald Hall, trailing by five points, had the ball at their own 8-yard line. It was third down, with only fifty-seven seconds left to play.

Klapper's first thought was that this did not interest him in the slightest, but a second thought occurred to him: *They'll never make it.*

He watched as the ball was snapped, and the entire Voles' big front line charged in at Cathy. Suddenly Bruno and Boots threw themselves into the path of the thundering Voles. They took quite a beating, but gave Cathy enough time to complete a pass to Larry Wilson, who ran out of bounds at the Warriors' 39-yard line to stop the clock. Time remaining: forty seconds.

"What pass protection!" Klapper exclaimed, but quickly clamped a hand over his mouth. He didn't care. So what if those boys were showing heroic guts and determination?

"I say, Klapper," called Mr. Sturgeon from his seat in the bleachers. "I understood that you did not approve of football."

"Well — uh — I don't," Klapper stammered, "I'm just — uh — visiting the old enemy, and — *Holy cow, what a handoff!* Tricked the whole defense!"

"Yes," agreed Mr. Sturgeon in amusement. "It's obvious that you're in no danger of showing enthusiasm here. Enjoy the game — or not, of course."

The clock was ticking down as the Warriors set up for the next play at the Voles' 41-yard line. Seventeen, sixteen, fifteen . . . they'll never have the time, thought Klapper, concentrating on the play while unconsciously crumpling up his report as his excitement built. The crowd was at fever pitch. If his football obsession wasn't all a thing of the past, he'd *swear* this was more exciting than watching the pros. The heart! The self-sacrifice! The desire!

With ten seconds to go, the play began. Klapper watched intently, and suddenly he was staring right at it — an open receiver with a clear path to the goal line.

"*Pa-a-a-a-ss!*" he shrieked hysterically, just as Cathy reared back and fired the long bomb. It sailed high in the air, and landed right in the hands of Sidney Rampulsky just inside the 20-yard line. Sidney grabbed the ball and headed home.

"*Don't fall!*" cried practically everyone on the Warriors' bench.

This distracted Sidney, and he jerked his head in the direction of the bench, causing him to lose his footing. He sailed gracelessly through the air, bobbling the ball wildly above his head, before landing face-first on the grass, just as the gun signified the end of the game. The ball, still clutched in his hands, rested just over the goal line. Touchdown: Macdonald Hall.

Pandemonium broke loose. The students of Macdonald Hall stood up on their seats and cheered, but Miss Scrimmage's girls did them one better; they rushed the field to carry the quarterback around on their shoulders. Sidney, flushed with victory, spiked the ball, and then tripped over it, banging his head on the goalpost. Miss Hildegarde had to rush out to attend to him. Henry Carson and Coach Flynn hugged each other joyously as the team celebrated on the sidelines around them.

Onto the scene barreled a wild-eyed Kevin Klapper, his hair and clothing in disarray, his mangled report still clutched in his fist. He threw himself at Carson and Flynn, practically knocking them over. "We did it! We did it! What a play! What a quarterback! *What a team!*"

Mr. Carson stared at him. "I thought you didn't like football!"

Klapper staggered back. "Don't like football? Me? I *love* football! It's more than a game! It's — everything! The world! Life!" Then he began to run around among the jubilant players, bonking the front of their helmets with his forehead. Eventually he wound up at the head of a snake dance started by Dave Jackson.

In the stands, Mrs. Sturgeon was dabbing at her eyes with a handkerchief while trying to calm down Miss Scrimmage, who was sobbing uncontrollably. Even Mr. Sturgeon was on his feet, applauding his students. Calvin Fihzgart was emotional, too. His teammates had won this game for him, to avenge his grievous injury.

Bruno and Boots ran up to Cathy. "Okay," said Bruno breathlessly. "Elmer's in the clubhouse ready to switch places with you."

Cathy scowled. "I did all the work, and he gets all the credit!"

"Come on," said Boots anxiously. "If someone tries to interview the star and finds out it isn't Drimsdale, Bruno and I are dead! We're the captains of this team!"

"Oh, all right!" she snorted, beginning to jog to the dressing room. "You guys have no spirit of fun!"

Finally order was restored so that Myron Blankenship could end the game officially by kicking the extra point. He missed it, because he was too busy talking about Steve Hadley's hangnails, but that still left the final score 37–36 in favor of Macdonald Hall.

Kevin Klapper's celebration had not ended, though. He was gamboling around the bench, congratulating everyone and singing victory songs — loudly, and rather off-key. Finally Coach Flynn pointed to Klapper's report, by this time crumpled, torn, and shredded around the edges. "What's that folder you've been carrying around?"

At first Klapper looked shocked. "This?" An enormous grin split his small face, and he ripped the report into tiny pieces and cast them into the cool fall breeze. "Nothing. Nothing at all."

7.
A
Pale
Flush

For the rest of the weekend, Macdonald Hall was in a festive mood. Henry Carson was so pleased by the Warriors' first victory that he ordered what was left of the truckload of zucchini sticks to be passed out during the celebration. For this reason, Bruno, Boots, and the rest of the Zucchini Disposal Squad made several trips to the clubhouse and the spare equipment room, where the four Manchurian bush hamsters were housed.

The Warriors were the center of attention, and gloried in it, all except Elmer Drimsdale. As the game's star, most of the congratulations were directed to him. To avoid quarterbacking questions, he retreated to the equipment room in the clubhouse, and spent the remainder of the weekend working with his bush hamsters.

"That's Elmer for you," shrugged Bruno at lunch on Sunday. "He'd rather be left alone with his rats and his chemicals and his ants and his machines. Still, wasn't that an incredible game?"

All at once an excited babble rose up at the table, and the game was replayed in words for the umpteenth time. The boys laughed about who dropped what pass, who missed which tackle, and who fumbled, fell, and, every so often, did something right. And, as always, the talk shifted to Cathy, who had turned it all into a win.

Boots rubbed his shoulder feelingly. "Yes. Cathy. Do you know how much I ache today from the hits I took so that no harm would come to Cathy?"

"The bottom line," said Bruno, "is that we're well on the road to the championship and our rec hall."

Wilbur peered over a large slab of apple pie. "The championship? Are you nuts? We squeaked out *one* game by a single point, at the last second, against the worst team in Ontario!"

"A challenge was given to us, and we met it," Bruno insisted. "So if we keep on doing that for the rest of the season, we win the championship, right? And don't worry, guys. Boots is working on a brand-new rec hall plan, so we'll have all the angles covered."

Calvin Fihzgart didn't suit up for practice on Monday. Though the pillowcase he used for a sling bore several prominent food stains, and the bandage of electrical tape was becoming dog-eared around the edges, Calvin clung to his compound fracture story.

On his sling he had printed in blood-red Magic Marker:

THE BEAST:

TEMPORARILY OUT OF COMMISSION

"I'm still on the injury list," he told Coach Flynn. "These things don't heal overnight!"

"Okay, Fihzgart," sighed the coach, more relieved than exasperated. "Sit it out until you — uh — recover."

The practice was led by, of all people, Kevin Klapper, who had traded his usual gray suit for sweatpants, warm-up jacket, sneakers, and coach's whistle.

"Team," he announced, "believe it or not, seventy-two hours ago I thought football was an evil influence. I thought it built slobs, not men, and I was actually looking down on Macdonald Hall because of it." He flushed, terribly ashamed. "All that is behind me. And I'm going to work with Mr. Carson and Coach Flynn to see to it that we turn the Warriors into the best team we can be."

"I thought that guy was some kind of education inspector," whispered Boots as Klapper raved on about the great future in store for the Macdonald Hall Warriors. "How'd he get to be a football coach?"

Bruno shrugged. "Maybe he got a promotion or something."

"I smell trouble," Boots insisted. "A normal guy with a job doesn't suddenly start coaching a football team. Remember, as captains, we're bound to get nailed if anything goes wrong."

"If this guy can help us win games, I'm all for it. Besides, how could anything be blamed on us? We don't even know what's going on."

It was the toughest practice of the year. Klapper led the team through two hours of exhausting drills that left everyone gasping.

"That new guy's a slave driver!" puffed Cathy. "This is no way to treat a lady!"

"Pardon me? What was that you said?" asked Myron Blankenship with great interest.

"None of your business, Blabbermouth," replied Bruno, glaring at him.

"Oh, well, in that case, did you know that Gary Potts — "

"We know," Bruno interrupted. "Thanks to you, the whole campus knows. The poor guy probably can't even go to class without someone checking for his dandruff, all because there's a blabbermouth on the loose at Macdonald Hall."

Myron looked unperturbed. "Well, you know how these rumors get around," he said, and jogged off.

After practice, Mr. Carson and Mr. Klapper walked together to their cottages on the south lawn.

". . . and we have to work up a playbook," Klapper was saying. "Especially defensive patterns. We're weak on defense — "

"But Kevin," Mr. Carson interrupted. "Where are you going to get the time for all this? We'd love your help — you know more about football than anyone I've met in a long time. But you've got a job. Aren't there other schools to inspect?"

Klapper stopped in his tracks. In all the excitement about the Macdonald Hall Warriors, he had completely forgotten his schedule. The Ministry expected him to finish here and move on. How could he work with the team if he was flitting from school to school all over the province?

Well, he wasn't *really* finished here, was he? His report had been damaged during the game. Why, he would need a week to redo it. Maybe two. It wasn't as though all education would grind to a halt just because of a week or two.

Aloud, he said, "I think I can stretch out my stay here long enough to do my part to help the team."

Carson shrugged. "Okay. I hope you know what you're doing."

"I'll see you at seven to start on the playbook," said Klapper.

The two men split up, each heading for his own cottage.

As Klapper opened his door, he heard the telephone ringing. Probably Mr. Greer, his superior at the Ministry of Education in Toronto. Klapper was due back today with his report, and Greer was probably calling to see what was holding him up.

He regarded the ringing telephone oddly for a few seconds, then strode determinedly to the wall and yanked on the cord. The jack popped out and landed at his feet. The ringing stopped.

He realized that he was backsliding on his promise to stay away from football, but how could he pass up the chance to work with these dedicated youngsters? With Hank the Tank Carson, the legendary linebacker of the Green Bay Packers? With Drimsdale, possibly the greatest little quarterback ever to play at the junior high level?

Still, he'd have to tell Greer something. He couldn't just drop off the face of the earth for two weeks. He regarded the telephone with distaste. Over the phone, he'd probably have to answer a lot of silly questions. He reached into his briefcase, produced a sheet of Ministry of Education stationery, and fitted it into his typewriter.

Dear Mr. Greer,
        For a number of reasons, I have been delayed here at Macdonald Hall. Please notify my appointments in the next few days that I will have to reschedule.
                              Yours very truly,
                              Kevin Klapper

He pulled the sheet from the roller and read it over with satisfaction. Yes, that pretty much said it all. Quickly he banged out an envelope, affixed a stamp, and took a stroll to the mail slot in front of the Faculty Building.

That took care of Greer. What about Marjorie? It was to his wife that Klapper had made the football promise. She would never accept that he was involved with football again.

He smiled. It wouldn't be too hard to keep all this from Marjorie. She herself said she found his job terribly boring. So he wouldn't burden her with the details.

In room 306, Bruno peered over Boots's shoulder at the recreation hall floor plan on the desk.

". . . and here we have the couches," Boots was explaining, "facing the TV; and over here we have two long tables and a bunch of chairs."

Bruno looked at him expectantly. "And?"

"And we can bring in some games. You know, chess, checkers, backgammon, Monopoly, cards, maybe Trivial Pursuit."

"You mean that's it?" cried Bruno.

Boots looked mystified. "What's wrong with it? We can go there, sit around, watch TV. . . ."

Bruno was appalled. "That's not a rec hall — that's a *barn*! I suppose we're going to stack bales of hay against the wall, and have a water trough and a pail of oats!"

"Listen, Bruno. Why do you think The Fish didn't like our first plan? Because he has something against wave pools? He isn't going to let us build Disneyland North. This is a good, reasonable plan."

"Reasonable!" snorted Bruno. "It's an empty room. Rec is short for recreation, you know. The closest thing to recreation a guy could get in this cave is boredom!"

"It's got a TV," argued Boots.

"Wide screen?"

"They cost thousands! Wave pools cost *hundreds* of thousands! I can't even guess how much spiral staircases go for! Your old plan would have set the school back probably over a million bucks. Sure, this isn't as fancy, but it gives The Fish nothing to complain about!"

"That's because there's nothing in it," Bruno retorted. "Forget it, Boots. You're my best friend, but we've got to face facts — you blew it. And now, just when it looks like we have the rec hall sewn up, we have no plan!"

"It was only one game!" said Boots. "Maybe it

was just luck! We'll probably never win another one!"

"Are you kidding? We're great! What can stop us?"

Cathy Burton was in a terrible snit. Wednesday morning at breakfast, Miss Scrimmage told her assembled students the wonderful news. This weekend, the whole school was taking a lovely field trip to Niagara Falls.

Cathy was so upset by these tidings that she couldn't eat her breakfast. With Diane in tow, she marched right up to Miss Scrimmage to complain.

"But Catherine," protested the Headmistress, "this whole trip was your suggestion."

"That was before the *Warriors*!" Cathy insisted. "We can't miss Saturday's game!"

"Now, Catherine, it's only one game. There will be so many others. And this will be such a pleasurable diversion."

Cathy was positively pale. "But the team needs us, Miss Scrimmage! Our — cheerleaders!"

The Headmistress smiled tolerantly. "I realize that we're enthusiastic supporters, but for this one game, Macdonald Hall will have to shift for itself." She chuckled. "It's not as though we're taking Elmer Drimsdale away from them."

Diane was overcome by a sudden fit of coughing.

"Please, Miss Scrimmage!" Cathy was pleading now. "Take everyone else, but leave me here! I can't miss that game! Honest!"

"Catherine, that will do. We are going to Niagara Falls, and we are having a lovely time, and that is that. Do you understand?"

* * *

Boots O'Neal and Wilbur Hackenschleimer were walking across the campus toward the stadium for football practice that afternoon, idly listening to the shouts from the girls' weekly croquet tournament. Suddenly there was a loud crack! and a yellow croquet ball came sailing high over the wrought-iron fence surrounding Miss Scrimmage's school. The boys watched as it bounced off the cab of a panel truck on the highway, and landed on the Macdonald Hall grass, rolling to a stop right at their feet. Boots bent down to pick up the ball. He stared. Over the yellow paint was printed in black India ink:

Field trip. Can't play Saturday. Sorry. C.B.

"So much for our rec hall," commented Wilbur.

They rushed into the stadium and showed the message to the team captain.

Bruno was outraged. "The *nerve* of that girl, blowing us off like this! And just when we were on a big winning streak, too!"

"Bruno, it's a field trip," said Boots defensively. "You know Cathy. If there was some way to get out of it, she'd have found it."

"Well, this is just *great!*" scowled Bruno. "Not only are we going to get killed on Saturday, but we have to figure out some way to explain why Elmer can't play."

They found Elmer in the stadium clubhouse, experimenting with the bush hamsters, using different multivitamins.

Bruno knelt beside the cage so that his face was

about half an inch from Elmer's. "Elm, you don't look so hot."

"Really? I feel fine."

"No, you don't," Bruno insisted. "You look pale. Right, Boots?"

"Right," said Boots uneasily. "And I think you're coming down with a fever."

Elmer frowned. "But then I wouldn't be pale. I'd have a flush."

Bruno looked him over carefully. "Yes, there it is — a flush. A pale flush. You work too hard, Elmer. It's exhaustion."

Elmer was offended. "I don't know what you're trying to tell me, Bruno, but I can assure you I'm in perfect health."

Bruno sat down on the floor and tickled the nose of one of the bush hamsters through the bars of the cage. "To tell you the truth, Elm, you're sick because you have to be sick. Cathy can't make it to the game on Saturday, so we need an explanation why the quarterback isn't playing."

Elmer looked panicky. "I told you this charade would get us all into trouble. Now what are we going to do?"

Bruno shrugged. "Nothing. You'll take to your bed in great misery, and when the game is over, you'll have a miraculous recovery."

Elmer was unconvinced. "But what if Miss Hildegarde comes to examine me and finds out that I'm not really sick?"

Bruno smiled. "Haven't you heard of the old glass-of-hot-water-under-the-bed trick? The nurse turns her back, you take a swig, and presto — 102°. Add

95

a little moaning and groaning, and you're sick as a dog."

Elmer folded his arms in front of him. "I'm sorry, but my work with the bush hamsters is too important. Every day is vital. I can't spare the time."

"Listen," argued Bruno, "if you don't fake sick on Saturday, when Cathy doesn't show up, everybody's going to find you, suit you up, and make *you* the quarterback! Understand?"

Elmer looked totally beaten. "How sick am I?"

Bruno awarded him a slap on the back. "Not very. Just a little flu or something. The change of scenery'll do you good."

The next day, Kevin Klapper finished planning the day's practice and updating the playbook before noon, and happened to be passing the office when Mrs. Davis, the school secretary, called to him.

"Mr. Klapper, someone named Greer has been looking for you all week," she said, handing him a stack of pink message slips. "He says he hasn't been able to reach you at your cottage number."

"Thank you, Mrs. Davis. I'll take care of it." Mr. Klapper headed away, his brow clouding as he leafed through the messages. Greer — Greer — Greer. What a persistent fellow. Obviously the letter hadn't been enough explanation for Klapper's absence. Now, here was a nuisance.

He continued to examine the slips. Greer — Greer — Greer — Carson? The bottom message was from Henry Carson, dated this morning, not forty-five minutes earlier, in fact. It read:

Drimsdale ill. Room 201. Urgent.

8.
Wrong-Way
Rampulsky

"One hundred and one point seven degrees," announced Miss Hildegarde, examining the thermometer. She, Coach Flynn, and Henry Carson were gathered around the bed where Elmer lay, trying to look suitably ill. The thermometer trick had worked, but he had burned his tongue on the hot water, so his discomfort was very real.

"Blast!" exclaimed the coach. "We can't risk playing him on Saturday!"

Elmer sat up in his bed. "I should really try to make it to my afternoon classes."

"You're *at* your afternoon classes, Drimsdale!" snapped Miss Hildegarde, "*and* your morning classes, *and* your evening classes, from now on until I say you're recovered! Got it?"

At that moment, Kevin Klapper came bursting into the room. "What's happening?"

"Drimsdale's out for Saturday," said the coach mournfully.

"Who's the backup quarterback?" asked Klapper.

Carson shrugged. "Nobody. We were using O'Neal. But he can't really pass. What do you think we should do?"

"Forfeit," moaned Coach Flynn.

"Everything's a learning experience," said Klapper seriously. "We can work on the running game and the defense. We'll do the best we can."

"And when Drimsdale comes back, we'll be more well-rounded," added Carson.

"Cut the strategy session!" barked Miss Hildegarde, beginning to push the three men towards the door. "The boy's supposed to recover, not listen to you talking about the game he's going to miss!" She threw open the door and pointed out into the hall. "Now, get lost!"

Outside the window, Bruno let go of the sill and crouched in the bushes beside Boots. "Guess what, Melvin. You're the quarterback again."

Boots made a face. "Don't they know how lousy I am?"

"Oh, sure. But we haven't got anybody else. Anyway, the important thing is Elmer pulled it off perfectly. Academy Award stuff."

The Warriors had a rough Saturday. Mark Davies' scoreboard read **GO WORRIERS** and that pretty much said it all. Even Bruno's lucky penny, kissed and rubbed until it was shiny, couldn't save the home team. On the very first play of the game,

Sidney Rampulsky grabbed the ball and ran forty yards in the wrong direction over his own goal line. There he stopped, spiked the ball in triumph, and an opposing player pounced on it for a touchdown.

Coach Flynn covered his eyes. "When he's going in the *right* direction, *he falls!*"

"Somebody should have told me," said Sidney reproachfully.

"We couldn't catch you!" cried Pete.

Myron Blankenship missed five field goals, and probably would have missed extra points, too, except that Macdonald Hall scored no touchdowns. He did manage to kick the ball holder twice. And for the last play in the first half, he missed the ball and holder altogether, sending his shoe sizzling between the goal posts. The other team applauded wildly. For the first time all year, Myron Blankenship had no comment. Macdonald Hall went to the locker room down 14–0.

Quarterback Boots O'Neal spent most of the game buried under a large pile of opposing players. After some frantic halftime coaching from Kevin Klapper, the Warriors began to put the offense together a little with some quick handoffs. They drove all the way to their opponents' 10-yard line, but then Wrong-Way Rampulsky struck again. This time, however, the Warriors were alert. Larry and Pete tackled Sidney around midfield. There Sidney fumbled, costing Macdonald Hall another touchdown. In fact, the only Macdonald Hall points in the game came when Wilbur and Bruno got tangled up, and the big boy fell backwards onto the opposing quarterback in the end zone for a safety. Final score: 21–2.

It was a much quieter Warriors team that slunk into the locker room after this less than sparkling performance.

"No grumbling," said Henry Carson cheerfully. "I don't want anybody blaming anybody else. It was no one's fault."

"Yeah, we all stank equally," said Dave Jackson morosely.

"And those end zones," Sidney complained. "They look exactly alike!"

Bruno was devastated. "I can't believe it," he said to the coaches. "You had such faith in us, and we let you down."

"Every team has to get a bad game out of its system," said Coach Flynn in a shaky voice.

"I wouldn't say that," said Kevin Klapper brightly. He produced a clipboard. "Last week we had thirty-six points scored against us; this week, only twenty-one. And they had the ball most of the game. Good work, defense." Half the team brightened. "And, sure, the offense didn't score, but we were pretty confused with our regular quarterback out. And at the end, a few of those ground plays were starting to click. All in all, this was a positive experience. Remember — as soon as a game is over, it may as well have happened ten thousand years ago. But next week's game is always only five minutes away."

Larry Wilson spoke up. "But you won't be with us next week."

Klapper looked mystified. "I won't?"

"Your job," Larry replied. "The Ministry needs you at another school, right?"

Klapper frowned. Why was it that, in the middle

of the most exciting, stimulating, and essential talk about football, someone kept bringing up the Ministry? "Oh," he said casually, "my work here isn't progressing as quickly as I'd expected, so I'll be here for at least another week."

There was a great cheer.

By the middle of the week, Kevin Klapper's continuing presence at Macdonald Hall had come to the attention of the Headmaster.

"Mildred," he said, sitting down at the kitchen table as his wife prepared to serve the meat loaf, "I'm afraid we have some more trouble brewing."

"Oh, William," she chided, setting his plate in front of him. "You can be such a crab sometimes. What is it now?"

"Kevin Klapper. He simply will not go away. We may have to adopt him."

Mrs. Sturgeon sat down at her own place. "Don't be silly, William. I'm sure there's a logical explanation for Mr. Klapper still being here."

"Oh, it's logical, but that doesn't mean it makes any sense," said the Headmaster, spearing a potato with his fork. "He's staying because of the football team."

His wife looked shocked. "I know Mr. Klapper despises football, but I can't believe he would take it out on our team."

"He isn't taking anything out on them, Mildred. He's coaching them."

She stared. "You *must* be mistaken."

The Headmaster shook his head. "Mrs. Davis says that his office in the Ministry calls at least five or six times every day. I'm positive that he either won't

answer his phone or has disconnected it. He's hiding out here, Mildred! We're harboring a fugitive from the Ministry of Education!"

"Are you sure he isn't perhaps a little behind in his work so he's forced to remain?" she suggested.

"How would that explain the fact that I just saw him at the stadium conducting a drill in pass defense? No, Mildred. The man has run amok over football again."

"If that's true, you must speak with him, William. People listen to you."

Mr. Sturgeon put down his knife and fork with a clatter, shaking his head vehemently. "I wouldn't touch this situation with the proverbial ten-foot pole."

"But you must!" she insisted. "The last time this happened, poor Mr. Klapper practically ruined his life!"

He nodded sadly. "And now he's out to ruin mine."

A miniature pink paper airplane sailed across the auxiliary guest cottage living room and nosedived into the wastebasket. There it lay, wings crumpled, amid the wreckage of many others, an entire day's worth of messages from Mr. Greer.

Kevin Klapper fitted a sheet of letterhead into his typewriter and sat down thoughtfully.

Dear Mr. Greer,

Just a little update on the many exciting things I'm doing at Macdonald Hall.

The geography program is excellent. Us-

long bomb pass, and the other after it bounced off Sidney Rampulsky's helmet. Myron Blankenship ended his field goal drought, which gave Macdonald Hall a big lead going into the fourth quarter. But the Chiefs, a middle school team from Niagara Falls, weren't ready to lie down and die so easily. They fought back with a vengeance. Macdonald Hall held on, and the last few minutes of play had Kevin Klapper, Henry Carson, and Coach Flynn jumping up and down on the sidelines, screaming encouragement at the defense, who were being pounded on every play. Finally when the gun went off, the score was 31–27, Macdonald Hall.

** ZICTORY ** proclaimed the scoreboard.

Elmer spent the game in the clubhouse in the spare equipment room, taking notes and experimenting with his Manchurian bush hamsters. Suddenly Cathy burst in, cleats clattering. "Okay, Elmer, you're on! Get in the shower, and by the time everyone else gets here, I'll be out of your equipment and gone!"

Meekly Elmer nodded his assent, and headed for the shower room.

"Hey," called Cathy, "aren't you going to ask how we did?"

"How?" rasped Elmer, his throat closing.

"We killed them," she grinned. "Tell Mr. Klapper he's a genius!"

So it was that when Mr. Carson led the jubilant team into the locker room, they found the quarterback's uniform and equipment draped over a bench, and Elmer, wrapped in a towel, just stepping out of the shower. The big ex-linebacker ran up to embrace him, but Elmer fled fearfully to the other side of the room.

"Drimsdale," said Carson lovingly, "you're one in a million!"

The celebration that night was even greater than it had been after game one. As Pete Anderson put it, "Let's face it. The first game was kind of a fluke, and last week we got killed. Today we *really* won!"

Across the highway, Miss Scrimmage's celebrated right along with them. Officially these were two separate parties, but that didn't stop Cathy and Diane from raiding the entire dessert section of Miss Scrimmage's kitchen, and sneaking it across the road to Bruno and Boots's room, where a number of boys were relaxing before lights-out.

The boys were eternally grateful. "Don't forget we're in the zucchini zone," Wilbur reminded them, setting to work on a large slab of chocolate fudge cake. "This is great," he added, his mouth full.

"It's the least I can do for my teammates," said Cathy grandly.

Diane looked around the room. Plates of zucchini sticks were piled on every available surface, including parts of the floor, in places stacked three or four high. She whistled. "How many orders of that stuff have you guys got?"

"With Hank the Tank, the sky's the limit," replied Bruno. "But don't worry. In a couple of hours, all this'll be gone. Who's on zucchini disposal duty?"

"Sidney just took the last batch down," Boots supplied.

"See?" said Bruno to the girls. "He should be back any minute. Then we send somebody else."

He indicated the zucchini plates with a sweeping gesture. "We're looking at two, maybe two-and-a-half more hours here. Our bush hamsters could eat the Faculty Building and everybody in it."

They waited, but Sidney did not come. Mark, Sidney's roommate, was the first to become edgy. Boots was next, but soon even Bruno was alarmed by the amount of time Sidney had been gone.

"Maybe he just met some guys and he's hanging out with them," Diane suggested.

Bruno shook his head. "We've got to go find him."

With Cathy and Diane following in the shadows, the boys marched out to the football stadium clubhouse. The door of the spare equipment room was open. Boots got there first, and gawked. "Bruno! Look!"

The rest of the group ran up to the door and stared. The bush hamsters' cage was mangled beyond recognition. The bars were badly bent, and the door was broken off. About three feet away lay Sidney, flat on his back, out cold.

Instantly Mark wet a towel and set about restoring his roommate.

Sidney's eyelids fluttered, and he sat up woozily. "Oooh! I had a little accident."

"What happened?" asked Bruno impatiently.

"I tripped over the cage," Sidney admitted, touching the bump on his head experimentally. "And I had a little trouble getting up, because there were zucchini sticks all over the place, and I kept slipping on them."

Diane looked around. "I don't see any zucchini sticks."

"That makes sense," said Boots. "The bush hamsters ate them before they — before they — " Suddenly his face drained of all color. "Bruno, the bush hamsters are *gone!*"

"Oh, *no!*" moaned Bruno. "When Elmer hears about this, he'll freak out!"

"*No-o-o-o!*"

Bruno swallowed hard. He had never seen Elmer this upset. "Don't worry, Elm. First thing in the morning, we'll go looking for them. We'll get them back to you."

"My head hurts," said Sidney plaintively.

"*Keep quiet!*" thundered Elmer in outrage. "This is all your fault, you — you accident-prone personage!" Purposefully he stepped around a small computer and began rummaging through his closet. "We must find those bush hamsters *immediately!*"

"It's five minutes to lights-out," protested Boots. "How can we look for furry little animals on a totally dark campus?"

"With infrared glasses, of course!" Elmer pulled out a small carton that contained several devices that looked like scuba-diving masks. "Everybody take one!"

"What are you doing with infrared glasses?" asked Larry in amazement.

"How else can one see in the dark?" Elmer responded.

"You've heard of a flashlight?" asked Wilbur.

Cathy fitted the rubber strap behind her head and peered out the window. The dark campus seemed perfectly visible through the infrared lens. "Hey, wow, these things are great! Everything looks

108

green, but it's light as day! I've got to get me a pair of these!"

Elmer was so agitated that his throat hadn't closed up, even in the presence of the girls. "No dallying! It's urgent that we find those animals!"

"Being out after lights-out is against the rules," Pete put in.

"*Rules?*" barked Elmer, approaching hysteria. "Four Manchurian bush hamsters — *an endangered species* — are on the loose, and you're telling me about *rules?* We're searching *now!* Glasses in place! Forward — march!"

With Elmer in the lead, they climbed one by one out the window, and regrouped outside the dormitory.

Pete scanned the large campus. "Where do we look first?" he asked helplessly.

"Everywhere," said Elmer firmly. "I calculate another eight hours and seventeen minutes until sunup. We have that long to retrieve the bush hamsters without any of the instructors finding out about it."

By midnight, the search party had split up, and the various groups were off in different corners of the campus, still awaiting the first sign of Elmer's bush hamsters. There were a few anxious moments when someone gave the regroup signal, an owl call, but that turned out to be a real owl. Further excitement was caused by Sidney's urgent cries, but that too was a false alarm. He was stuck up in a tree where he had chased a squirrel, thinking it was a bush hamster.

Bruno, Boots, Cathy, and Diane were combing the area nearest to the highway.

"I could *kill* Sidney Rampulsky for this!" Boots was muttering. "I mean, why can't we just go to school like everybody else? Why are we always burying zucchini sticks, or looking for bush hamsters, or something?"

"Maybe it's your punishment for being such a complainer," said Bruno absently, creating a gap in the bushes with his arms, and gazing inside.

"Don't you realize how boring life would get if stuff like this didn't happen?" Cathy asked Boots.

"Boring?" Boots repeated. "It would be great not to have to look over your shoulder half the time to see if The Fish is there."

"Speaking of looking over your shoulder," said Diane nervously, "who's that coming out of your dorm right now?"

Boots gazed at the figure through his infrared glasses, and went white to the ears. "It's Hank the Tank!"

Bruno folded his arms in front of him in consternation. "He figured we'd all be partying on the night of the game, so he held a bed check! He's getting to be a pretty sneaky guy, you know!"

"What are we going to do?" asked Diane.

The four watched as Mr. Carson paused thoughtfully outside the dormitory entrance, then headed for the highway. They ducked behind some bushes as he jogged across the road and scaled the wrought-iron fence surrounding Miss Scrimmage's Finishing School for Young Ladies.

"He thinks we're at Scrimmage's!" exclaimed Bruno.

"He's not stupid," said Cathy. "Remember last time?"

Suddenly in the distance, a voice declared, "*Halt!*"

"It's Miss Scrimmage!" Boots hissed, beginning to panic. "She's got Hank the Tank!"

"We've got to save him!" declared Bruno. "Call the guys! Give the owl signal!"

"I don't know how to hoot like an owl. Why don't *you* give the signal?"

"I thought it up, Boots. That doesn't mean I can *do* it."

Cathy threw up her hands in disgust. "Oh, you guys are hopeless!" She began to hoot vigorously, the sounds echoing all across the deserted campus.

"But Miss Scrimmage," explained Henry Carson breathlessly, "I was just looking for my team! I wasn't terrorizing anybody!"

"Keep those hands up!" barked the Headmistress, gesturing at him with her shotgun. "Two of my girls are not in their room! Where are they?"

"Honestly, Miss Scrimmage, I don't know. I was just — "

"I know precisely what you were *just*!" she snapped. "These eyes may not be as young as they used to be, you know, but I recognize you perfectly, young man. You're Henry, the awful thug from Macdonald Hall who assaulted me!"

Mr. Carson was sweating now. "I'm sorry about that," he mumbled. "I thought you were going to hurt my team."

"You're *sorry*?" she shrieked. "A huge man like yourself attacking a poor, defenseless old woman

111

trying to protect her innocent young girls!" She gestured across the highway. "Come along. We're going to see Mr. Sturgeon. *He'll* make you tell me where my students are!"

He moaned. "Aw, you don't want to go there. It's after midnight. I'll tell you what — put away the gun, and I'll help you look for your girls."

"No tricks, Henry. Now, march!"

So it was that when the Manchurian bush hamster search party assembled in answer to Cathy's call, they were greeted by the sight of Henry Carson being marched across the road at gunpoint.

"Mr. Carson!" groaned Bruno in true pain.

"What are we going to do?" asked Pete.

Wilbur looked at him as though he had a cabbage for a head. "Nothing, of course. That's a *real gun* she's holding."

Bruno squared his shoulders. "Well, I'm going over there."

Boots stared at him. "To do what?"

"To confess. This is our fault. Hank the Tank wouldn't have gone to Scrimmage's if we'd been in our rooms for bed check. Now, who's coming with me?"

There was a painful silence.

"Come on," Bruno prompted. "You don't expect Boots and me to go alone, do you?"

"Me?" squeaked Boots. "Who volunteered me for the suicide mission?"

"We'll go," said Cathy, despite much signaling from Diane. "Maybe we can calm Miss Scrimmage down."

One by one, the boys all agreed to join the expedition. Even Elmer, still frantic over his bush hamsters and terrified by the prospect of being caught outside after lights-out, allowed himself to be talked into it.

"Good," said Bruno. "Now, here's the plan. We form a big circle around Hank the Tank and Miss Scrimmage, and then we close in on them. When Miss Scrimmage notices us, we confess that it's all our fault, the Tank goes free, and we take the rap."

"Great plan," said Larry without enthusiasm. "I *love* taking the rap. Maybe we'll even get to rake more leaves."

Bruno nodded. "I know it's a bummer, but we owe it to the Tank after all he's done for us. Okay, let's go."

"The next time you have a bush hamster search," Wilbur told Elmer as the group scrambled off after Miss Scrimmage and Mr. Carson, "issue bulletproof vests."

The Headmistress was marching her prisoner toward Mr. Sturgeon's cottage on the south lawn, and the search party caught up with them almost halfway there. The students had no trouble forming a large ring around the pair, and then shrinking the circle exactly according to Bruno's plan.

Mr. Carson noticed them first, but since none of the students had remembered to take off the infrared glasses, he saw only a ring of masked intruders. "Hey, look!"

Miss Scrimmage wheeled and, spying the beggogled prowlers, drew up in horror. "A street gang!" she screamed, and fainted.

"Who are you people?" Carson demanded.

Elmer was the first to unmask. A loving grin split Henry Carson's gruff face. "My quarterback! He came to save me!"

Cathy and Diane ran up to their fallen Headmistress. "Miss Scrimmage!" cried Cathy. "Speak to me!"

Mr. Carson was holding a joyful reunion with his players. "You don't know how good it is to see you men!" he crowed.

"Aren't you mad because we were breaking training?" blurted Pete.

"All I know is I was in trouble, and *my team* rescued me!" He pointed to the goggles. "Where'd you get these nifty disguises?"

"Well," Bruno began, "we were — oh, you don't really want to hear this, do you, Mr. Carson?"

Miss Scrimmage was just coming to. "Catherine — Diane. Thank goodness you're safe. There's an awful street gang in the neighborhood — terribly rough-looking juvenile delinquents wearing the most hideous sunglasses!"

Quickly Cathy tossed her infrared mask, along with Diane's, over to Boots. "Let's go home, Miss Scrimmage, okay?"

The Headmistress nodded vaguely.

"She'll be fine," whispered Diane to Boots. "Don't worry about Miss Scrimmage. She's the Iron Lady."

Henry Carson glanced over to where the girls were helping Miss Scrimmage sit up. "Oh, no! She's up again! I'd better get out of here before she sees me! Get some sleep, men."

Elmer looked totally downcast. "My bush hamsters are *gone!* Now they'll never reproduce!"

* * *

But Elmer was wrong. The bush hamsters were not gone. They were safe and sound under the north bleachers of the Macdonald Hall football stadium, feeding contentedly on the thousands of unwanted zucchini sticks thrown there during that afternoon's game.

The four animals munched themselves a comfortable nesting spot amidst the zucchini sticks. It was big enough for a family, which was important. After all Elmer's experimentation and testing, the secret to breeding Manchurian bush hamsters lay in the combination of spices in the Mr. Zucchini batter. The two females were each expecting a litter in a week's time.

9.
Under
Contract

The next morning found Bruno and Boots seated in the outer office in response to a summons from the Headmaster.

"I can't figure out why The Fish wants to see us," said Bruno in perplexity. "We haven't done anything lately."

Boots emitted a nervous laugh. "We haven't, eh? So soon you forget. What about last night?"

Bruno shrugged. "The Fish couldn't know about that. Even if Miss Scrimmage squealed, Hank the Tank was the only person she saw, and he'd never turn us in."

Mr. Sturgeon opened his office door and invited them inside. Instinctively they seated themselves on the hard wooden bench directly across from the

Headmaster's desk — Macdonald Hall's hot seat.

"Walton, O'Neal — allow me to regale you with a little tale. At one o'clock this morning, I received a telephone call from Miss Scrimmage. It was difficult to put together her story exactly, but it had to do with a double kidnapping masterminded by Mr. Carson, and a marauding street gang, whose members all, for some reason, were wearing sunglasses in the middle of the night."

Bruno grinned in spite of himself. "But sir," he said carefully, "what does this have to do with us?"

The Headmaster smiled back, a dangerous smile. "The two kidnappees were Miss Burton and Miss Grant. You will forgive me for immediately thinking of you two as soon as their names came up."

Bruno fell silent. Boots emitted an audible gulp.

"So you will now explain to me the events of last night, and put my mind at rest. Shall we start with the street gang?"

"That was us, sir," Bruno admitted. "We were celebrating the game yesterday, and it went kind of late. That's why you can't blame Hank the — uh — Mr. Carson. When we weren't in our rooms for his bed check, he went to look for us at Scrimmage's because of — last time."

"But we weren't there," put in Boots quickly. "We were still on campus."

"How admirable," said the Headmaster sarcastically. "No doubt Miss Burton and Miss Grant were joining in the festivities. I don't suppose you'd care to furnish a list of the other merrymakers." There was dead silence. "I thought not."

"So it's pretty straightforward," Bruno concluded. "Miss Scrimmage caught Mr. Carson and was taking him over to your place. So we were going to confess, but Miss Scrimmage thought we were a street gang, and passed out."

"And the sunglasses?" Mr. Sturgeon prompted.

"Oh, right. Well — remember Elmer's Manchurian bush hamsters? The ones you wouldn't let him keep in the dorm? They got lost, so Elmer gave us infrared goggles so we could look for them in the dark."

The Headmaster sat forward in alarm. "And did you find them?"

"Well, no. Miss Scrimmage messed everything up. But we'll keep looking."

"Do that, Walton," sighed Mr. Sturgeon, feeling rather uncomfortably that this was his fault. "Please tell Drimsdale that I shall notify the local authorities to be on the lookout for them as well. You are dismissed."

Gratefully Bruno and Boots scurried off.

The Warriors had the afternoon off, so Kevin Klapper traveled to Toronto to take his family to the zoo. Klapper had been away for some time, and was making a concerted effort to spoil his children, as he had missed them very much. Any food, toy, or souvenir they wanted was instantly theirs.

Marjorie Klapper watched the family reunion fondly. She was used to her husband being out of town so often, and was grateful to him for making the two-and-a-half-hour drive to Toronto to visit her and the children.

Finally Karen and Kevin, Jr., ran ahead into the monkey house, leaving the two parents alone.

"Kevin," Marjorie began, "I've been getting some

strange phone calls from your boss, Mr. Greer. What exactly are you doing at this Macdonald Hall?"

"My job," said Klapper absently. "I don't talk about it, because I know how much it bores you." He pointed into the monkey house. "Look at Karen in front of the orangutan cage."

"But Kevin," Marjorie persisted. "Mr. Greer says you're not supposed to be at Macdonald Hall anymore. And he says you don't answer his phone calls."

He looked surprised. "I've written him twice to tell him exactly what I'm doing. What's *wrong* with the man?"

His wife looked worried. "Mr. Greer said your last letter barely even got to him. He said it made no sense, and most of it was covered with food. He's very anxious about you, Kevin."

He put his arm around her shoulders. "Everything is fine, Marjorie. I'm really enjoying my work at Macdonald Hall. Look at me. Have you ever seen me so relaxed and happy? I'll straighten everything out with Greer. I'm sure it's a simple misunderstanding. He has a very important job, you know, and he's under a lot of pressure. Now, come on. Let's grab the kids and go get some cotton candy."

"Fihzgart," said Coach Flynn at Monday's practice, "I've talked to Miss Hildegarde, and she says there was never anything wrong with you. It's been over two weeks now. Are you on the team or what?"

"Of course I'm on the team," growled Calvin, whose arm was still taped up and bent at the elbow in the pillowcase-sling. "I'm just on the mend, Coach."

The coach threw his hands up in exasperation.

"What about our next game? Are you playing?"

Calvin patted his wounded arm gingerly. "You know I want to, Coach. But if I get hit hard before my compound fracture heals all the way, it could be a career-ending injury."

Mr. Carson called everyone together for a team meeting. "Men, we're on the road this week against Kingston Junior High. We're going to drive to Kingston in the morning, play the game, and stay overnight in a motel near the school."

Bruno and Boots exchanged looks of pure agony. An uneasy murmur passed through the team. Would they have to play another game without Cathy?

"I know the bus ride is a pain," put in Klapper, "but that's football."

"We've got mostly home games because ours is one of the best stadiums," Mr. Carson added. "It won't kill us to go out of town this once."

As they headed for the clubhouse, Boots sidled up to Cathy. "Now what?"

"There is *no way* I'm missing this game," replied Cathy's voice from behind the frames of Elmer's glasses.

"Maybe she could stow away on the bus," mused Bruno thoughtfully.

"Are you crazy?" cried Boots. "What if one of the coaches saw her?"

"Maybe we could tell them the truth, and they wouldn't mind," suggested Bruno. "They know how great she is."

"If you guys are finished . . ." said Cathy sarcastically. "How about I convince Miss Scrimmage to take the cheerleaders to Kingston?"

"She'd say yes?" asked Bruno in disbelief.

120

"Of course not," Cathy replied. "But when the whole school lays a guilt trip on her because of the game we lost, she might change her mind. It's worth a shot, anyway. See you." She ran off into the clubhouse.

Boots watched her jog away. "She really runs that school," he commented in awed respect.

Bruno nodded. "Oh, yeah."

As soon as it was officially announced across the road that Miss Scrimmage intended to take The Line of Scrimmage to Kingston for the game, Bruno and Boots went to see Elmer Drimsdale.

Bruno knocked politely on the door of room 201. "Hi, Elm. It's us. Can we come in?" He pushed the door open, and he and Boots entered.

The room was a sea of boxes. Elmer had crated up all his experiments and machines and stacked them in small pyramids around the room. The chemistry lab was gone, too, replaced by a huge carton bearing labels reading DANGER: KEEP AWAY FROM HEAT, DANGER: CORROSIVE, and DANGER: DO NOT AGITATE. In fact, the only thing that wasn't in some type of box, besides Elmer's school books, was the battered empty cage that had once held the bush hamsters. It was at this that Elmer was staring, seated on his bed, the picture of despair.

"What hit this place?" Boots blurted out.

Elmer looked up from the cage. "I haven't had any interest in my other experiments ever since the bush hamsters disappeared."

"Come on, Elm," argued Bruno. "What's one little foul-up? Think of all the great stuff you've done!"

Elmer shook his head. "I could make machines

121

and chemicals do what I wanted them to, but when it came time that an endangered species needed my help, I let them down."

"*Not* true!" insisted Bruno. "Those bush hamsters took off on *you*, remember? You didn't open up the cage and say, 'Hey, rats, hit the road!' Besides, you'll have them back any time now. The Fish told the police, and put notices in all the local stores, so the whole countryside's looking for them. And all the guys are, too, because Dave told the Blabber-mouth." Elmer looked unconvinced. "Anyway, Elm, we can't think about that now. Another crisis has come up, and Macdonald Hall needs your help."

"What kind of help?" asked Elmer suspiciously.

"Well," began Boots, "the football team — "

"*A-ha!*" screamed Elmer. "From now on I'm having nothing to do with your football team. If it wasn't for that team and its victory party and its zucchini sticks, my bush hamsters would still be here today!"

"But you haven't even heard what you have to do yet," Bruno protested.

"I'm not interested. All year you've needed my *help*, and all year I've been miserable." He folded his arms in front of him. "No."

"But Elmer, it's important. Miss Scrimmage thinks she's bringing ten cheerleaders to Kingston. The extra one is Cathy — "

"I'm not listening," interrupted Elmer.

"So on the field there'll only be nine, because Cathy will be playing. And Miss Scrimmage may not be too bright, but she can count. And let's face it, Elm. You have nothing to do during the game, so I just thought — "

Elmer pointed a long, bony finger right into Bruno's face. "You want me to be a cheerleader!" he accused.

"A wig, maybe a little makeup, and nobody would know the difference," Bruno reasoned. "It would fix everything. Because if Miss Scrimmage sees only nine cheerleaders and thinks she's lost a girl, she'll raise a big stink, and we'll get found out."

Elmer's face turned purple. "I am bowed down with disbelief! The fact that you could ask me to do this *proves* that you are not a human being!"

"Elmer, I'm pleading! Look! I'm begging!" Bruno got down on his knees. "Do this one last thing, and I'll never ask you for anything again as long as I live!"

Elmer looked disgusted. "If I thought you meant that — "

"I do! I do! Boots is our witness! Honest! Never again!"

From his desk, Elmer produced a sheet of Canadian Horticultural Society stationery, and wrote:

> I, Bruno Walton, hereby certify that
> upon completion of prescribed
> cheerleading duties by Elmer Drimsdale
> on November 7 of this year, I will never
> again ask said E. Drimsdale to help me
> or anyone or anything else, nor try to
> recruit him for any purpose, so long as
> we both shall live.

Bruno signed readily, and Boots gave his signature as a witness. Elmer took the paper and clutched it to his heart.

Bruno looked annoyed. "Remember, if you

123

chicken out on us, it's a breach of contract."

Boots grabbed his roommate by the collar. "Shut up, Bruno. Let's quit while we're ahead."

The bus carrying the Macdonald Hall Warriors left at eight o'clock Saturday morning. The trip was a lively affair. Elmer was in great spirits the whole way, laughing and joking, and showing off his contract with Bruno.

"Favoritism," muttered Wilbur darkly. "Why can't *I* get one of those?"

"Keep your voice down," said Bruno irritably. "If the Blabbermouth finds out about this, we're dead."

"I've never seen Elmer so happy," remarked Pete.

"Yeah, well, I've got a theory about that," said Boots worriedly. "When the bush hamsters disappeared, I think he went a little nutty. Do you know he packed up all his experiments?"

"I didn't mean to let those bush hamsters loose," said Sidney, who had felt horribly guilty ever since the incident. "It was an accident."

"No one's blaming you, Sidney," said Larry soothingly. "Any damage you cause goes down as an act of nature, like an earthquake, or a tidal wave."

They arrived at eleven-thirty. Miss Scrimmage's group was already there, since the Headmistress drove the school minibus personally, averaging eighty-five miles per hour the whole trip. She had trouble converting speed limit signs out of the metric system.

The Kingston Junior High Kings played in a local high school stadium, not nearly as modern as the

Macdonald Hall facility, but with seating for over a thousand spectators.

The Warriors were warming up and stretching, and the cheerleaders were setting up for their opening routine when the tenth member of the Line of Scrimmage took the field.

"Ohhh!" groaned Dave Jackson. "Those cheerleaders are embarrassing! They're terrible! Check out the red-haired one with the bow legs. She looks like she can't even see where she's going!"

Boots grinned nervously. "Look closer, Dave."

Dave squinted at the redhead and goggled. "It's *Elmer*! Elmer without his glasses! Man, he makes an ugly cheerleader!"

Elmer, dressed in a Line of Scrimmage uniform, a gaudy red wig that positively glowed in the chill November sun, makeup and eye shadow liberally slopped on his face, was barreling wildly around the sidelines. Without his glasses, and wearing shoes a size and a half too tight, he was out of control, bouncing off the other cheerleaders as though he were caught amidst the bumpers of a pinball machine, pom-poms flailing wildly.

"Elmer, *calm down!*" ordered Wilma Dorf, the head cheerleader.

Elmer couldn't hear her over the sound of his own voice screaming, *"Yay, team, go, team, go!"* He was fiercely determined to be the best cheerleader on the field, so that Bruno could never say he had failed while under contract.

The start of the game was delayed because the Kings were bowled over in amazement, and the Warriors were laughing too hard to kick off. Bruno and Cathy in particular were half collapsed in hysterics by the 30-yard line, holding onto each other for support. Boots stood near them, saying, "Sure. Go ahead and laugh. What are we going to do if he *kills somebody*?"

"Wow!" exclaimed Mr. Carson as Elmer blindly decked Ruth Sidwell and continued his rampage on the sidelines. "Who's that?"

Mr. Klapper shook his head. "I wish we had her for the defense."

Finally the game began, and the other cheerleaders managed to quiet Elmer and sit him down. Soon, though, the Kings fumbled, and Macdonald Hall recovered, and Wilma hauled Elmer to his feet so the cheerleaders could do their usual celebration.

"Way to go, team! Number one! Yes!" He began a mad dance, darting around like a grasshopper in a jar. An errant hand clouted Wilma on the jaw, and the other cheerleaders dropped to the ground to avoid his flailing arms.

"What are we going to do?" one referee asked the other.

The man shrugged helplessly. "Is it legal to penalize a cheerleader for unnecessary roughness?"

Stepping on Wilma's leg, Elmer staggered out onto the field. The crowd rose to its feet in a standing ovation, and Bruno and Boots grabbed Elmer and dragged him to the sidelines. There was a loud chorus of booing from the stands.

"Elmer, you've got to mellow out!" Boots exclaimed frantically.

Elmer rubbed his eyes, smearing his mascara into large black rings that made him look like a raccoon. "I can't see anything! And my shoes are too tight!"

"Try not to be so violent," coached Bruno. "And don't yell so loud."

"Oh, no you don't!" said Elmer belligerently. "You're trying to make me do a bad job so you can tear up the contract!"

"Just cool it!"

They led Elmer back to the other cheerleaders, amid tumultuous applause, and jogged back towards the play.

The first half of the game turned out to be a defensive battle, with neither side able to produce a touchdown. Cathy had thrown several perfect passes, but the Macdonald Hall receivers were having a tough day, dropping almost everything that came their way. As the half neared its close, with the score still 0–0, the crowd became bored and restless.

Suddenly someone started to chant, "We want the redhead!" until it caught on, and soon the whole stadium rang with, *"We want the redhead! We want the redhead!"*

In a panic, Boots nudged Bruno. "They're calling for Elmer!"

His red wig a fiery blur, Elmer rocketed off the cheerleaders' bench to a huge ovation. He opened his mouth and bellowed:

"Two—Four—Six—Eight, Whom do we appreciate?"

"YOU!" the crowd roared back.

Macdonald Hall used its last remaining time-out to get Elmer off the field.

In the second half, the Kings came out flying, taking the lead 14–0, and things were looking grim indeed for Macdonald Hall.

"I hope you've got a speech to explain why *this* is a positive experience!" groaned Coach Flynn to Kevin Klapper as Dave Jackson let a pass slip right through his extended hands.

"All we need is one big play," said Klapper anxiously. "Then everything's going to start clicking. I can *feel* it."

No sooner were the words out of his mouth than an unlikely hero emerged for Macdonald Hall. With an offhand remark about Gerald Hoskins' chronic bad breath, Myron Blankenship jogged onto the scene and kicked an almost impossible long-distance field goal.

From that moment, the Zucchini Warriors took over. Cathy threw two touchdown passes to make the final score 17–14 in favor of Macdonald Hall. The Warriors were ecstatic, and even the Kingston fans were not disappointed, as they were treated to the sight of Elmer Drimsdale's victory dance, which brought the house down.

There was no Mr. Zucchini outlet in Kingston, so the team feasted on a victory dinner of hamburgers while the community newspaper interviewed quarterback Elmer Drimsdale about his two spectacular fourth-quarter touchdowns. Mr. Carson sent them to bed early.

"There," said Bruno, adjusting the hotel room thermostat with the edge of his lucky penny. "The knob part's broken off, but it's okay now. Hey, Boots, what's eating you?"

The two were preparing for bed in their tiny room at the Olympiad Motel, not too far from Kingston Junior High.

Boots was seated on his bed, looking unhappy. "It's Elmer. You saw him today. He was like a Mexican jumping bean with lipstick! Think about the Elmer we know — dull, quiet, meek. I think we pushed him too far and messed up his personality."

"I know what you mean," said Bruno thoughtfully. He threw on his jacket over his pajamas. "So let's pay Elmer a visit — you know, to see how he's doing. Just watch out for Hank the Tank."

Barefoot despite the cold autumn night, the boys padded past the ice machine to the room Elmer was sharing with Pete Anderson. They knocked softly, and entered.

The entire Kingston Junior High cheerleading squad sat cross-legged on the floor with Elmer, sharing a huge pepperoni-and-mushroom pizza. Elmer was in the middle of a play-by-play description of his brilliant field generalship, while Pete sat on his bed, staring in amazement.

"Hey, Elm," said Bruno. "What *is* this?"

"A few people who appreciate good football and fine Italian food," said Elmer.

In the background, Pete shrugged expansively.

"You're the greatest quarterback in the world," one of the girls told Elmer. "But you've got to get rid of that redheaded cheerleader. She's got legs like a piano."

"And she's crazy!" added another vehemently.

"I assure you that she will not appear again," said Elmer, looking meaningfully at Bruno, and patting his back pocket, where the folded contract was safely tucked away.

Boots leaned over to Bruno. "Pssst! I thought his throat closes up when there are girls around."

"I think he's cured."

"Well," said Elmer to Bruno and Boots, "have a good sleep. See you on the bus tomorrow."

Bruno was in shock. "He hoofed us out!" he exclaimed, as he and Boots made their way back to their own room. "I can't believe it's Elmer!"

Boots grimaced. "Let's just hope he gets back to normal soon."

10.
The
Glory
and
the
Pizza

While the Zucchini Warriors were covering themselves with glory in Kingston, a blessed event took place under the north bleachers of the Macdonald Hall football stadium. The two female Manchurian bush hamsters gave birth to litters only an hour apart. By morning, forty-one baby bush hamsters were munching happily on the castaway zucchini sticks. The babies looked like miniature versions of the adults, except for the mane of long hair framing the parents' heads. That would grow in about three weeks. It took only that long for a newborn bush hamster to reach full maturity.

The four parents watched carefully, making sure none of the babies strayed beyond the enclosure of the bleachers. This watchfulness was not necessary.

It seemed that newborn bush hamsters were every bit as fond of the taste of deep-fried zucchini sticks as their parents were.

But with the large new number of mouths to feed, and no home football game in over a week, the food supply was quickly dwindling. So the two fathers ventured forth from under the stands to seek out a new source of nourishment for their growing families. Their keen noses soon led them to a large garbage bin outside the Macdonald Hall kitchen, where the pickings were excellent.

They were sampling the scrapings from last night's lasagna when two sets of human hands reached down to grab them. Hair standing on end, the bush hamsters took off at top speed, but the humans followed and chased them. . . .

". . . around the corner of the Faculty Building, and right along the front driveway," finished Mark Davies. "And, let me tell you, those little guys can *move*. Chris and I were gasping."

Bruno and Boots were back in room 306, catching up on their homework late Monday afternoon when Mark came by to tell them about his encounter with the bush hamsters.

"Did they get away?" asked Bruno.

Mark nodded. "We chased them halfway to the moon! Chris had to stop in the middle because of his foot."

"What's wrong with his foot?" asked Boots.

"Ingrown toenail," Bruno told him. "Haven't you been listening to your local blabbermouth lately?"

"Then those speed demons ran me into the ground. But it's good news anyway, right? It means hours a day. "Bruno and Boots are so scared that I'm going to get killed that they're turning into fantastic linemen. Dave is a good receiver, and Sidney would be great if he wasn't such a klutz. Larry, Wilbur, Pete, and those guys are punching up the defense. And the Blabbermouth is amazing everybody!"

Diane snorted. "When I first started at Scrimmage's, I was expecting a lot of things. But being the roommate of a football hero was *not* one of them."

"There's only one thing that worries me," said Cathy, sobering suddenly. "Mr. Klapper. What if he has to leave us and go back to Toronto?"

That question was on everyone's lips. As a celebrating Warriors team clattered into the locker room after their fourth win of the season, very suddenly the talk and laughter stopped, and all attention focused on the curriculum inspector/coach. There was a heavy silence.

Finally Henry Carson got up the nerve to ask everybody's question. "So, Kevin — uh — got any plans for next Saturday?"

Mr. Klapper looked perturbed, and lapsed into deep thought. No one spoke. No one even moved. At last the answer came: "Well, my report isn't quite finished yet. And then there's the typing and proofreading — " The rest of his remarks were drowned out by a lusty cheer.

Boots snuck out to the bushes behind the clubhouse where Cathy was hiding, awaiting this week's news. "He's staying!" And Cathy scampered happily across the highway.

That week, Kevin Klapper mailed several prog-

they're somewhere around the campus."

"Right," agreed Bruno. "Let's go tell Elmer. Maybe a little good news will bring him back down to earth."

Elmer wasn't in his room, but a neighbor said he'd gone into town with one of the faculty and his wife on a shopping trip, and was due back shortly.

Bruno frowned. "Elmer doesn't shop."

"After the last few days," said Boots fervently, "I'd believe you if you told me he was growing a tail! *Nothing* would surprise me."

He was wrong. At that moment, Elmer appeared at the end of the corridor. Both boys gawked. The person they were looking at bore no resemblance to Elmer Drimsdale, school genius. He looked like the cover of *Funky Beat* magazine. His normal crew cut had been plastered to his head at the sides and fluffed up on the top, hanging over his forehead as much as was possible with Elmer's short hair. His glasses had been tinted to look like shades, and reset into slick metallic-blue frames. He wore a patterned jacket with the collar turned up and the sleeves rolled to the elbows. His shirt was silk, his tie leather, and blue-and-white suspenders held up incredibly baggy wool pants. This arrangement Elmer completed with a pair of pink high-top sneakers.

"Elmer!" gasped Bruno. "What happened to you?"

Elmer looked highly insulted. "Nothing 'happened,' " he said stiffly. "It just occurred to me that, since I'm a star, I should see to it that I *look* like one."

"Come on, Elmer — *think*!" Boots pleaded. "You're not the star! Cathy is!"

Elmer glared at him. "When the game is over, who do the newspapers interview? Who gets the glory and the pizza?" There was no answer. "Exactly," he said with satisfaction.

"Well, anyway, Elm," said Bruno, "we've got great news for you. Mark spotted a couple of your bush hamsters on campus."

"I am the most important person in junior high school athletics," said Elmer simply. "I have no time for such things."

"But what about your experiments?" Boots blurted out.

"Ah, yes, the experiments. That Elmer Drimsdale doesn't exist any longer. I have a duty to my public." With that, he brushed by them and disappeared into his room, baggy pants flapping.

> *Dear Kevin,*
>
> *I am writing because I cannot seem to reach you by phone. I am deeply concerned about what it is that has been keeping you at Macdonald Hall for so long. Your letters tell me very little, except that you are involved in some sort of special project.*
>
> *I must insist that you telephone me immediately so that we can discuss this problem.*
>
> *Yours sincerely,*
> *Douglas Greer,*
> *Curriculum Supervisor*

Klapper read the letter morosely. It looked as though his days were numbered. He would have to go back to the Ministry to get sent on some dull

134

assignment, leaving behind his Warri initely his heart. And just when the t him most, just when everything was l click, just when Macdonald Hall was in tion for a play-off spot.

Of course, even if he left this minute he'd arrive at the office with no report would never stand for that. So he'd l report — and these things took tim through Saturday. He relaxed. And a was here over Saturday, he may as wel game.

He glanced at the date and hour c watch. Greer wanted him to phone in. excellent time for that, because right would be away at his weekly meeting w ister of Education.

Quickly he reconnected his phone Greer's secretary. "Hello, Loretta. Ke here . . . oh, not in, eh? What a pity. V him I called as he asked me to. Tell h is coming along, and I'll be in touch d Thank you, Loretta. 'Bye."

He hung up and disconnected the pleased with himself.

In the weeks that followed, the Mac Warriors' game began to take on a ne caught passes suddenly outnumbered ones. No longer was it common to see a Hall defender standing flat-footed mouthed as an opponent danced elega him for a touchdown.

Cathy was flushed with excitement

ress reports to Toronto — in Latin, since that was the course at Macdonald Hall he was supposed to be working on. Loosely translated, they were four different recipes for jalapeño bean dip. He also took Henry Carson along on one of his visits home, and the two had a pleasant dinner with Marjorie and the children.

Still, on Saturday, when the Warriors won their last game of the regular season, clinching a play-off spot, the question remained: How long could Kevin Klapper stay?

"We're in the play-offs! But we shall not stop there! We shall do everything, destroy everyone, and win the championship!"

This was coming from Elmer Drimsdale, perched atop a dining-hall table, haranguing the lunchtime crowd. The students cheered wildly, except for the group in the corner. Elmer's friends sat at their usual table, looking on glumly.

"He's become a complete idiot," observed Larry sadly.

"And his outfits!" added Mark. "Look at those pants! Some poor zebra must be running around naked!"

"I want the old Elmer back," moaned Boots. "I can't stand to see him like this." He threw up his hands in despair. "I can't stand the glare from his clothes!"

"Don't worry, guys," said Bruno. "It can't last any longer than the football season. Pretty soon he'll be tinkering with some experiment. His bush hamsters might even be back by then."

"Fat chance," said Mark. "No one's seen them since the day they ran me ragged. They're capital-G Gone."

"Well, if nothing else, this says a lot for how far the Warriors have come," said Bruno. He pointed to where Elmer was being lovingly escorted to a table of admirers. "We started from scratch, and now everyone associated with the team is big news. Face it, guys. We're stars."

"Oh, come on!" said Boots in disgust. "We won a few games, half by luck, and half by Cathy. She's the real star."

"Football is a team sport," Bruno lectured, "so all her teammates must be stars, too."

"I'll buy that," came Wilbur's voice from behind a stack of veal cutlets. "I've always wanted to be a star. Have you seen the restaurants those guys get to eat at?"

"Weird," observed Larry, his eyes on Elmer. "He's been the smartest guy at the Hall since the day he got here, and he doesn't get popular until people think he's a quarterback."

"I don't know how they can expect us to show any enthusiasm for class with the play-offs coming up," complained Bruno as he and Boots walked down the hall of the Faculty Building after lunch. "I mean, who can get into history when there's history in the making? Hi, Perry."

Perry Elbert grinned broadly. "Hi, Bruno. How's that lucky penny of yours?"

"Fine," said Bruno oddly, continuing down the hall. He turned questioningly to Boots. "How does Perry know I have a lucky penny?" Boots shrugged.

138

A little further on, Kevin Brown was walking with Gary Potts. Passing Bruno and Boots, Kevin tossed over his shoulder, "Hey, Bruno, don't forget to shine up your lucky penny for the play-offs." Laughter could be heard all the way down the corridor.

Bruno stopped in his tracks. "I don't get it."

Just then someone in a passing group of students called out, "Hey, Lucky, where's your penny?" This was followed by assorted cackles and guffaws.

"Okay," said Bruno, looking around like a cornered gunfighter. "Who's the wise guy who's been making such a big deal out of my lucky penny?"

At that moment, from around the corner, an all-too-familiar voice announced, "Hey, did you guys know that Bruno Walton has a lucky penny?"

"The Blabbermouth!" chorused Bruno and Boots. They raced around the bend and looked on in horror. There, surrounded by a small group of students, was Myron Blankenship, launching into a description of Bruno's lucky penny. Dave Jackson was on the scene as well, trying to quiet his roommate.

"It's a cheap imitation-silver four-leaf clover with a penny in the middle," Myron informed everyone. "And it's *ugly!*"

"Shut up," pleaded Dave.

Bruno was furious. "All right, who told the Blabbermouth about my lucky penny?"

Boots flushed. "I've been meaning to say something about this, Bruno — "

Bruno staggered back. "*You?*"

"I was telling Dave about how you used it on the thermostat in our hotel room in Kingston. I didn't see the Blabbermouth until it was too late!"

"And he keeps it with him on the bench at all the

football games," Myron was elaborating to his audience.

"Okay," said Bruno, calming down. "We need a logical, clear-headed plan to stop this." He looked thoughtful for a moment, then suddenly bellowed, *"Kill the Blabbermouth!"* and made a headlong dash into the crowd of students, hands outstretched towards Myron's throat.

"Bruno! *No!*" Boots managed to get a grip on his roommate's arms and hold him back.

"Hi, Bruno," Myron greeted him. "We were just talking about you."

"Let me go!" Bruno commanded. "The world will be better off!"

"You can't kill him!" pleaded Dave. "He's the only kicker we've got!"

Bruno relented. "Okay," he sighed. "But as soon as the season's over, *that's it!*" He looked threateningly at Myron.

"See you later," said Myron blithely.

"Mildred, do turn off the television."

Mrs. Sturgeon sat in front of *Monday Night Football*, watching enraptured. "I'm just trying to brush up on my football, dear. The play-offs are coming up. I want to know what I'm looking at when our boys are out there."

"I can tell you that easily enough," said the Headmaster grimly. "You'll be looking at Kevin Klapper losing his job."

"Whatever do you mean, William?"

"His superior phoned me today — a Mr. Greer. He wants to know why it's taken Klapper over seven weeks to do a simple assessment on Macdonald Hall."

"Oh, goodness!" Mrs. Sturgeon exclaimed. "Did you tell him that Mr. Klapper's been coaching football, and that he's absolutely indispensable to the team?"

Mr. Sturgeon sat down and let out a long sigh. "It's all very complicated, Mildred. I absolutely refuse to turn the man in, because I don't want Macdonald Hall to be caught in the middle of a war within the Ministry of Education. So I suggested that perhaps he should take the matter up with Klapper himself. And then he began yelling at me all about letters covered in food, disconnected telephones, and jalapeño bean dip, whatever that is."

She frowned. "How odd."

"Klapper is considered one of the Ministry's top people. But there is no doubt in my mind that if he doesn't report to his office soon, he will not have an office to report to."

Mrs. Sturgeon looked unhappy. "I do hope nothing awful happens to poor Mr. Klapper. The boys adore him. And except for this tiny problem with the Ministry, football has been such a wonderful experience for everyone."

Mr. Sturgeon groaned aloud. "Not everyone, Mildred. I saw a ghost today on our campus — a 'cool dude,' walking around looking like he just might have once been Elmer Drimsdale. You never saw anything like it in your life. It defies description."

Mrs. Sturgeon's eyes widened. "Did you speak to him about it?"

"I certainly did. And he explained to me that he was the most popular person in the school, and therefore must keep a high profile."

"Well," his wife said thoughtfully, "it's probably difficult for Elmer to adjust. To live so quietly for so long, and then suddenly to find the hopes of the entire school riding on your shoulders can't be easy."

"That's another thing troubling me," said Mr. Sturgeon. "I still find it difficult to believe that the timid, awkward, brilliant boy I've come to know at Macdonald Hall is the poised, agile athlete we see on the field. But do you know what bothers me most? When I mentioned the search for his bush hamsters, he flat-out told me that he has no interest at all in where they are."

Under the north bleachers of the Macdonald Hall football stadium, the colony of bush hamsters continued to flourish. The success of the Warriors had led to larger turnouts for the games. That meant more zucchini sticks, most of which ended up tossed under the seats.

The combination of spices in the zucchini batter was so healthy for the bush hamsters' metabolism that the two litters were growing up even more quickly than normal. Elmer's original four animals were soon to become grandparents. The babies were going to have babies.

11.
Arnold the Stuffed Hyena

Play-off fever swept Macdonald Hall. In only their first year of existence, the Warriors had qualified, along with seven other teams, to vie for the Daw Cup, the Ontario championship trophy.

"I want every guy in this school making a big fuss over the play-offs!" proclaimed team captain Bruno Walton. He needn't have bothered.

Editor Mark Davies published a special edition of the school paper, including play-off predictions, and a foldout poster of quarterback Elmer Drimsdale.

Art classes at Macdonald Hall devoted their energies to the production of Warriors banners and signs, and the school band began work on several new songs to celebrate the team's glory. Pep rallies were held. Across the road, the Line of Scrimmage experimented with more elaborate routines.

Bruno and Boots also started a poster campaign, encouraging the students to bring creative noise-makers to the games — everything from trumpets and cowbells to garbage can lids and spoons. Football was on everyone's lips.

Students could be seen running imaginary plays on notebook pages, using X's and O's as players. The boys were speaking knowledgeably of screens, blitzes, encroachment, clipping, and double coverage.

As the interest in the Warriors swelled, so swelled the head of Elmer Drimsdale. He had completely lost touch with reality, and was totally into the part of number 00. To him, the fact that he was not actually playing quarterback had nothing to do with his fame. He spent all of his spare time circulating among the students, making speeches, sharing in students' food from home, and autographing endless copies of his foldout posters for boys to send to their sisters.

The real Macdonald Hall Warriors were far too tired to enjoy their fame because of Kevin Klapper's new practice schedule. By now, Henry Carson and Coach Flynn had stepped aside to let the master work, and were acting only as assistants.

"You know," said Carson, standing on the sidelines during one of the many heavy drills, "I've had eleven years in the pros, and I've never seen a coach like that."

Pete Anderson looked on nervously. "What if he has to leave?"

Carson suppressed a shudder. "If he does, we can't hold it against him. The man has a job, and a family to support."

"You mean you don't know about Bruno Walton's lucky penny?" said Myron Blankenship incredulously to the ball holder for kicking drill. "He rubs it for luck, just like it was a rabbit's foot. And once it got into a rummage sale by mistake, but he bought it back."

Bruno flew through the air and hit the tackling dummy like an express train.

"Nice hit, Walton," Klapper called. "That's putting your heart into it."

"I'm pretending it's the Blabbermouth!" muttered Bruno under his breath.

The message was short and to the point:

KLAPPER — GET BACK HERE
IMMEDIATELY OR ELSE. — GREER

He had been staring at the telegram all day, mulling it over all evening. And now, one-thirty in the morning, he had reached a decision. There was no putting Greer off any longer — no more notes and messages. It was time to be honest. It was time for a meaningful gesture.

He reconnected his phone, and dialed the number of a twenty-four-hour florist in Toronto. There he placed an order to have a potted fern and ivy plant delivered to Mr. Greer's office at the Ministry. The card would read:

With deepest apologies, Kevin Klapper

145

That said it perfectly. He *was* sorry. But he was committed now. Win or lose, he was staying with the Zucchini Warriors until the very end. And Greer would have his apologies, and a very nice plant to brighten up his office.

Heedless of the hour, he rushed over to the guest cottage and pounded on Henry Carson's door. After a long while, a bleary-eyed Carson appeared before him, his bulky frame wrapped in a Mr. Zucchini bathrobe.

"Kevin! What are you doing here? It's two o'clock in the morning!"

"I'm staying!" Klapper announced joyfully.

Suddenly Carson was fully awake. "Staying? But what about your job?"

"I've taken care of that!"

"You mean you've squared it with your boss?"

"Well — I sent him a plant."

Carson swung the door wide. "I promise you, Kevin — you'll never regret this. Come on in. Let's have some cocoa."

On Saturday, the bleachers were jam-packed with umbrellas. The rain had started Friday evening, pouring all night, and had settled at dawn into a dreary cold drizzle. This set the stage for game one of the Daw Cup play-offs.

Within five minutes of the opening kickoff, it was impossible to tell one team from the other. Everyone was mud from head to toe. The game had to be stopped several times so the officials could hose off the ball. More than one pass, for both sides, was thrown to an opposing player, because all the jerseys

146

were now the same color — brown. Every tackle was a mud shower, every fall a slide, every catch a miracle. By halftime, the field looked like the Everglades.

"How is he?" asked Coach Flynn in the clubhouse.

A dazed and filthy Sidney Rampulsky sat propped up against his locker, spitting mud in all directions.

"He'll be okay," reported Larry. "He swallowed a lot of turf, though."

"Great play!" approved Mr. Carson. "He slid all the way into the end zone on his face!"

"It was worth it!" gurgled Sidney. "I got a touchdown!"

By the time the teams returned for the third quarter, the rain had stopped, and a thick fog had rolled in. This was great news for Macdonald Hall, who had the lead, 7–0. Offense was impossible for both teams, since no one could see to catch or get a foothold to run. The clock did the rest.

"Mildred, I must be out of my mind!" exclaimed a totally drenched Mr. Sturgeon as he and his wife navigated their way home through the mist. "Why did I allow that mud bath to continue? It will be a miracle if no one comes down with pneumonia!"

Mrs. Sturgeon wrung out her hat, laughing, "Oh, William, how can you think about pneumonia? We won!"

Shortly after the end of the game, the first litter of Manchurian bush hamster grandchildren was born. The second litter came the following morning, and by Monday's practice, the north bleachers of the football stadium were home to a community of one hundred and twenty-six.

Not twenty yards away from where grueling practices were going on all week, blessed events were taking place in the world of a no-longer-quite-so-endangered species. By the time a capacity crowd filled the Macdonald Hall football stadium for Saturday's semifinal matchup, the grand total of Manchurian bush hamsters was two hundred and seven. By the end of the game, there were twenty-one more.

The newborns were a little nervous, because the noise coming from the stadium was deafening. The game was a real barn-burner for the Warrior fans. They cheered themselves hoarse as the home team opened up a commanding fourteen-point lead in the first half, and then screamed in agony as the visitors roared back and caught up in the second. With the score tied 24–24, the Zucchini Warriors were going into overtime.

"Look," said Klapper, as players and coaches alike panicked around him. "The Panthers are more experienced than we are, and they've been going like a steamroller for the last thirty minutes of play. If this overtime goes long, we have no chance."

"What do you want us to do, Mr. Klapper?" asked Bruno.

"Three plays," said Klapper evenly. "That's all we can afford. Jackson runs back the kickoff, Drimsdale throws long, Blankenship kicks a field goal. That's all we need. First point wins."

Coach Flynn had been white as a sheet ever since the start of the second half, when the lead had begun to slip. "How can it work?" he whispered frantically as the teams took the field for the overtime kickoff. "These are just kids! Sure, they've come a long way and they've won some games. But you can't expect them to pull off a combination like that in an overtime of a semifinal game!"

Then the coach watched goggle-eyed as everything happened exactly the way Klapper had laid it out. Before he knew it, Myron Blankenship was jogging out to attempt the field goal.

There was dead silence in the stadium. Watching mesmerized from the bench, Bruno brought out his lucky penny and began rubbing it fervently. The snap was made; the holder teed up the ball. But instead of kicking, Myron pointed to the sidelines and announced, *"Look! There it is! His lucky penny!"*

A great gasp went up in the stadium from two thousand throats. On the field, the Warriors' line struggled to keep the Panthers from breaking through. The ball holder began to tremble, looking to the coaches for some kind of instruction.

At that moment, Cathy Burton leaped up onto the bench and let out a bloodcurdling shriek that was heard from one end of the campus to the other.

"KIIIIIIIIIICK!!!"

Myron looked startled. "Oh — yeah." He turned, ran up to the ball, and booted it dead center between the goalposts.

Final score, 27–24. The Warriors were in the championship game.

"Okay, Larry," said Bruno. "Let's hear the scouting report."

The weekend celebrations were over, and Bruno,

149

Boots, Larry, Wilbur, Sidney, Pete, Myron, and Dave were packed into room 306.

From his pocket, Larry removed a small notebook and flipped it open. "The Montrose Junior High Maulers," he began. "The best-ever team at our level in Ontario. The 1985, '86, and '87 Daw Cup champions. In all that time, they only lost one game, and that was by default, because of a chicken pox epidemic at their school. So far this year, they haven't won by less than thirty points." He looked up from his notes. "They have articles written about them like a dog has fleas, and they all say the same thing — *nobody* can beat these guys."

"They haven't met Cathy yet," said Bruno smugly.

"Yeah, but their quarterback's no slouch, either," said Larry. "The whole team is twice our size, faster, and ten times as strong. They've got this kid, Craig Trolley — he's thirteen years old, and he's six feet three, two hundred and thirty pounds. He cuts down quarterbacks like crazy!"

"I don't like the sound of that," said Boots nervously. "Our quarterback is — " he spied Myron " — you know — our quarterback."

"Hah," said Larry, "we've got no chance against these guys anyway. Without — our quarterback, it would be a joke!"

"I guess second place is a really great showing for a team in its first year," said Pete philosophically.

"Wait a minute!" interrupted Bruno, scrambling to his feet. "Who said anything about second place? This is Macdonald Hall we're playing for, not some two-bit school. Does Mr. Klapper deserve second place after the time and work and loyalty he's given us? Does Hank the Tank deserve second place after all he's done for us? Does the coach? Does The Fish?"

"The Fish deserves second place," said Wilbur pointedly. "He could have shown a little more mercy back on zucchini-burying night."

"Okay, so maybe The Fish," admitted Bruno grudgingly. "But just look at you guys! We haven't even taken the field yet, and you've got the game lost and our quarterback hurt. If we build the Maulers up in our minds like this, by Saturday we'll be too psyched out to play our best game. Sure, they're great, and they haven't lost in years — they're way overdue. They're *bound* to lose this one!"

"Bruno's right," said Pete. "We've come too far to give up without a fight."

"More than a fight! A *war!*" cried Bruno. "I'm *positive* we're going to win because — because — " He slapped his knee. "Because it's right and just!"

"And you want a rec hall," added Boots.

"That's something to keep in mind, too," agreed Bruno. "Okay, guys. Any questions?"

"Can we see your lucky penny again?" piped Myron.

Bruno looked at him severely. "You never learn, do you? I want you to know, oh Blabbermouth of the world, that if you had missed that field goal, you would not only have *seen* my penny; you would have had it wedged permanently up your nose!"

"It's almost lights-out," said Boots quickly. "See you guys at practice tomorrow."

Dave lingered after the others had gone. "Sorry

about my roommate and the lucky penny thing," he told Bruno. "Out of all his subjects, I think you're the new favorite."

"Why does he have to have any subject at all?" asked Boots.

Dave shrugged expansively. "Why? Why is the sky blue? Your guess is as good as mine. I mean, for a guy who sleeps with a teddy bear, he sure likes to open — "

Bruno sat bolt upright. "A *teddy bear?*"

"Well, not technically," said Dave. "It's really a stuffed hyena, but it looks a lot like a bear. It's named Arnold."

"And he sleeps with it?" prompted Boots.

"Every night. What's the big interest?"

Bruno and Boots exchanged a look of pure delight.

The hallway of the Faculty Building was filled with students during class change on Monday morning, and Myron Blankenship was on his way to Canadian history when Bruno and Boots appeared at the end of the corridor. Bruno was holding the school's electric megaphone. With a grin of triumph, he flicked it on, put it to his lips, and announced, *"Your attention, please! Attention, everybody! I just want to make sure everyone knows that Myron Blabbermouth sleeps with a teddy bear!"*

At first, a great laughing cheer went up in the hall, followed by a heartfelt round of applause directed at Myron, who stood there, horrified.

"Actually," Bruno went on, *"it's a hyena, seventeen-and-a-half inches in length, medium brown, black button eyes, yellow ribbon around neck. Very cute. He calls it Arnold."*

152

"Stop that!" snapped Myron.

"He usually sleeps with it under his right arm, except when he sleeps on his back. . . ." He switched the megaphone off to regard Myron, who had moved in, glaring. "Yes? You have something to say?"

"You know, Bruno," said Myron angrily, "it's really not very nice to talk about my personal stuff in front of all these people."

Boots could keep silent no longer. "I can't believe you! You've said something embarrassing about practically every guy in the school! You've got no complaints about this!"

Myron defended himself. "It's not *my* fault news travels fast."

"It sure does," said Bruno. "And I'm going to see to it that the news of your teddy bear travels to every corner of this campus — *unless* you promise to stop spreading stories about guys."

"What stories?" Myron demanded.

"Stories about hangnails, bad breath, who's in love with who, body odor, ear wax, *lucky pennies*, and all that stuff. Now, do you promise?"

Myron looked totally defeated. "I promise," he said, "but what about — ?"

"No," Bruno interrupted. "No personal stuff about any of the guys can cross your lips, or Arnold becomes big news. Do we have a deal?"

Myron grimaced. "Oh — okay."

"Fine." Bruno switched the megaphone back on. *"Attention again. You'll be pleased to know that Blabbermouth has just promised to give up his blabbering ways."* There was a big cheer. *"We now return you to your regularly scheduled classes."*

* * *

153

Under the north bleachers of the football stadium, bush hamsters were constantly being born, day and night, all through the week that led up to the Daw Cup game. The final litter of twenty-one was born during Thursday's practice — less than forty-eight hours before the championship game was scheduled to begin.

It had been ten weeks since Bruno's zucchini disposal squad had fed the first stick to the first bush hamster, and now Elmer's original four animals had given birth to a thriving bush hamster community under the north bleachers — population four hundred and fifty-one.

It was a little before lights-out on Friday night when Bruno and Boots came back from the last-minute meeting/party at the spare cottage.

"I can't believe Sidney bled all over Mr. Klapper's place!" exclaimed Boots, shutting the door of room 306. "I wonder how it happened."

"Didn't you see?" asked Bruno. "He just grabbed a handful of pretzels, turned, and walked right into the wall. And you know Sidney's nose. Once it starts bleeding, it's like Niagara Falls!"

"Well, anyway, it was really nice of Mr. Klapper to give us a little party *before* the game," said Boots. "You know — win or lose."

Bruno scowled. "What do you mean 'or lose'? The Warriors are awesome!"

"Come on, Bruno. You know we're not exactly favored to win tomorrow. We're playing a team that's undefeated by everything except chicken pox!"

"We can do anything we put our minds to," said

Bruno firmly. "Now, let's go to bed. If we don't get enough sleep tonight we'll waste all our energy on the game and have none left for the victory celebration."

Boots sighed. "Elmer was right," he said, crawling into bed and pulling the covers over his head. "You're not a human being."

"Cathy?"

"Yeah?"

"Are you asleep?"

"How could I be? You've been waking me up every five minutes."

Diane got out of bed and switched on the overhead light. "Well, I'm nervous! I've got pregame jitters!"

Cathy sat up in bed, annoyed. "You're not the one who's playing tomorrow, remember? I am."

"But aren't you scared?" asked Diane.

"Nope."

"See?" she said triumphantly. "You're too crazy to be scared, so I have to be scared for you." She began to pace the floor.

"Will you just quit crabbing and go to sleep? At this rate, I won't be able to keep my eyes open tomorrow, much less play."

"But what about Craig Trolley?" cried Diane. "The six-feet-three, two-hundred-and-thirty-pound guy on the other team? What if he hits you?"

"Then I'll fall down," yawned Cathy. "That's part of football. You don't become a swimmer if you're afraid to get wet, right? Now go to sleep."

"I *can't!*" Diane quavered.

"Well, then, keep pacing. But turn the light off.

And try to step quietly. I've got a big day tomorrow. I'm taking the Zucchini Warriors to the top!"

It was after three in the morning when Mr. Sturgeon suddenly sat bolt upright in his bed. "Catherine Burton!" He switched on the bedside lamp and shook his wife vigorously. "Catherine Burton is the quarterback of the Macdonald Hall Warriors!"

She turned over, still asleep. "That's nice, dear."

The Headmaster slammed his fist into his palm. "I can't believe I didn't think of it sooner! In my *soul* I always knew it couldn't be Drimsdale! Mildred, you're not listening!"

"Tell me in the morning," she murmured, turning over again.

Mr. Sturgeon plumped up his pillow and sat back against it, eyes blazing. The evidence was all there. Miss Burton, hooligan and troublemaker par excellence, had been quiet and low-key all year, which meant she had to be up to something. She was approximately Drimsdale's height and build. And Mr. Sturgeon had distinctly seen her get on the bus to Kingston, even though she was *not* a cheerleader.

"Turn the light off, William," Mrs. Sturgeon mumbled.

His head was spinning. If he thought back to the week when Drimsdale had been too ill to play, would he find that to be the weekend of Miss Scrimmage's trip to Niagara Falls? Of course! And that earsplitting scream that had come from Drimsdale's uniform when the Blankenship boy wouldn't kick the ball! All week he'd been wracking his brain over which of the students would be capable of such a sound. But it had been the Burton girl — then, and all along.

Did the coaches know? Impossible. Even Henry Carson would not be party to such a deception. The team certainly knew. And between the lax discipline at Scrimmage's and the help of boys like Walton and O'Neal, that dreadful girl would have no problem coming and going as she pleased. "Drimsdale" *did* always leave the field early.

It was positively brilliant — and completely unethical. And now that he had discovered the ruse, what was he going to do about it?

12.
The
Return
of
The
Beast

Saturday noon found Mr. Douglas Greer, curriculum supervisor of the Ontario Ministry of Education, in his car, driving east out of Toronto. His destination: Macdonald Hall, and Kevin Klapper.

All morning Greer had been unable to relax, bits and pieces of the past weeks dancing in his head — his unreturned phone messages, the bizarre food-covered letter, Klapper's phone call when he knew Greer would be out, those crazy Latin bean dip recipes. And finally — the last straw — that meaningless, ridiculous plant. A *plant*, of all things!

Greer sped up. Monday would be nine weeks since the day Klapper had been due to check in at the Ministry. *Nine weeks!* Greer couldn't believe he'd let things go this far. But who could have predicted that the staid and steady Klapper, his top curriculum inspector, would have gone completely crazy like this? So the weeks had rolled on, leaving Greer looking like an idiot, with no inspector, and no answers.

That was when it occurred to him: If he wrote a letter firing Klapper, he'd be depriving himself of the pleasure of firing him in person and seeing his reaction firsthand. Greer was secretly hoping Klapper would be difficult so he could have the extra bonus satisfaction of taking his potted fern and ivy arrangement and breaking it over Klapper's head.

In the end, though, Greer had left the plant in his office, since it looked so great there. In the event of trouble, a punch in the nose would substitute nicely.

"William, get out of bed. There's nothing wrong with you."

The Headmaster was sitting up against his pillow, arms folded stubbornly in front of him. "I am ill, Mildred."

"It's almost time for the game!" she protested.

Mr. Sturgeon worked up a small, dry cough. "I am not well," he insisted. "Go without me."

His wife was angry. "You think I don't know what's ailing you, William? You have that crazy idea in your head that Catherine Burton is playing quarterback for Elmer. You feel it's your duty to prevent her from playing, so you're lying low!"

"That's not it at all," he denied. "I fail to understand why a man cannot take sick without an act of Parliament."

"But there's nothing to worry about! That quarterback couldn't possibly be Catherine." Her husband pulled the covers up to his neck and coughed again. She pleaded, "Inspect the lineup yourself, if it will put your mind at rest!"

He set his jaw steadily. "If I did that, I'd risk infecting my students with — the ailment I have contracted. Here I am and here I stay."

She left in a huff, shaking her head and calling him childish. The instant he heard the front door click shut, he whipped out the remote control from under the covers and switched on the TV set to the channel that was televising the Daw Cup game. *His boys* would be on there in a few minutes, and he was going to cheer himself hoarse in the privacy of his own bedroom.

As for the Burton affair, he would investigate like a good Headmaster. Tomorrow. Today he was ill.

The Macdonald Hall parking lot had been full since ten o'clock, and cars were parked on both sides of the long driveway and on the highway shoulders in both directions as far as the eye could see.

It was a perfectly clear day, and the bright sun gleamed off the polished metal tops of a ring of Mr. Zucchini wagons surrounding the jam-packed football stadium like a train of covered wagons.

Inside, the thirty-two hundred seats were already filled, and a thick crowd of spectators framed the field on the sidelines.

The only Macdonald Hall or Miss Scrimmage's student not at the stadium was Elmer Drimsdale, who was holed up in his room, waiting for his cue. The game had attracted not only the students plus the local community support, but also a good many parents and alumni, coming from as far away as Montreal and Buffalo. A lot of Montrose Junior High boosters were in attendance as well, numbering in the hundreds.

The Macdonald Hall students were a lively group, wildly waving their signs and banners, and creating as much racket as was humanly possible on home-made noisemakers. One group near the front had rigged up seven vacuum-cleaner hoses to part of an old broken tuba. With one boy blowing in each hose, the sound was like a small earthquake. As fortune would have it, they happened to be sitting directly behind Miss Scrimmage, and the first time the seven played their instrument, she fainted. Diane Grant had to revive her with smelling salts. Actually Diane felt like fainting herself, but for a different reason. In a few short minutes, Cathy would be out there on the field playing against the toughest team in Ontario.

Not much was said in the Warriors' locker room before the game started. Mr. Klapper gave the play-ers a few last-minute pointers, and then a heavy silence fell. The boys sat staring at the coaches and each other until it was obvious that everyone was equally terrified. Then Mr. Carson said, "Let's play football!" and the squad clattered out of the clubhouse.

As they reached the turf, the Warriors found themselves staring into a television camera. Sud-denly a clean-cut sports reporter barked, "Do you have a comment on the game?" and thrust his mi-crophone in front of a player at random. It was My-ron Blankenship.

"I'm not allowed to say anything," came Myron's

whiny voice in response. "I made a promise."

The Warriors got a ten-minute standing ovation from the crowd, including a blast from the seven-man vacuum-cleaner tuba that raised Miss Scrimmage six inches out of her seat and had Diane rummaging for the smelling salts again.

Dave Jackson ran back the opening kickoff about five yards. He was stopped by the Maulers at the Macdonald Hall 15. Dave's family, who had driven in from Buffalo, cheered madly from the front row. The offensive team jogged on from the bench.

"They aren't so tough," Dave called to them. Then he saw number 56, Craig Trolley. "Some of them."

"He's the size of an adult," breathed Boots.

"An adult gorilla," Bruno agreed.

"Three of Wilbur at least!" exclaimed Larry.

Craig Trolley was definitely a man-sized thirteen-year-old, but at six feet three, and two hundred and thirty pounds, he was bigger than most men. He was also quick, and agile, with none of the clumsiness of many big boys.

"And all this time I thought buildings couldn't walk," said Cathy cheerfully. "Okay, line up."

The ball was snapped, and Cathy faded back to look for her receivers. Suddenly the two Mauler linemen separated, revealing Craig Trolley charging after the quarterback.

"Get him!" cried Boots.

Desperately he and Bruno stepped into the path of the big linebacker. Number 56 hit them like a freight train, plowing them backward into Cathy, and then hurling himself on top of the three of them, landing with a resounding crunch. The play was whistled dead.

Boots felt a finger tapping on his shoulder pad. Still dazed, he looked up to find Craig Trolley staring down at the pileup in great concern.

"Are you guys okay?" Craig asked, his face open and sincere.

"Yeah, thanks," said Boots.

Craig helped the three of them to their feet, and jogged back to the Maulers' huddle. Then he did exactly the same as before, sacking the quarterback, only this time he dragged Larry into the pileup as he threw himself on Bruno, Boots, and Cathy.

"Sorry about that," said Craig earnestly, giving the four fallen Warriors a hand getting up.

"Don't worry about it," breathed Boots. He turned to Bruno and Cathy. "We're all going to die."

"That guy's amazing!" said Cathy, rubbing her shoulder gingerly. "He's a cross between King Kong and Miss Manners!"

Marjorie Klapper was watching a terrible movie. It was the story of a sheepdog who was struck by lightning, developed an I.Q. of 180, and went around solving crimes for the F.B.I. In exasperation, she began flipping through the channels. On six there was a football game, and she was just about to turn the selector again when she heard the announcer's voice mention Macdonald Hall.

"That's where Kevin is!" she exclaimed aloud.

"So far the Macdonald Hall offense has been completely ineffective against Craig Trolley," said the commentator.

"Yes, Herb," the announcer agreed, "the Maulers are in complete control. Unless the Warriors can stop Trolley, they have no chance of getting into the rhythm of the game. The Macdonald Hall coaches seem baffled."

The screen showed a shot of Flynn, Carson, and Klapper looking on grimly from the sidelines.

"Kevin!" Marjorie shrieked. Aha! This was the reason for his prolonged stay at Macdonald Hall! This explained his crazy behavior! This was why Mr. Greer seemed so bewildered! Kevin Klapper was back on football. Only this time it wasn't enough for him to watch it. No, this time he had to coach! And at a school he'd been sent to by the Ministry, no less!

With a snort of contempt, she turned off the television set and went to look for Karen and Kevin, Jr. They were in the kitchen, hitting each other with soup ladles over who would get the last Twinkie.

"But I was winning!" protested Kevin, Jr., as Marjorie loaded him and his sister into the car.

"Where are we going?" asked Karen.

"To see Daddy," her mother replied, pulling out into traffic with a squeal of burning rubber.

Both children cheered. "I can't wait!" said Kevin, Jr., excitedly.

Marjorie's knuckles whitened on the steering wheel. "Neither can I!"

As the first half of the Daw Cup championship game neared its close, the Macdonald Hall football stadium had become a very quiet place. Most of the signs and banners were resting on the bleachers; the homemade noisemakers were silent; and the

bench between Bruno and Boots, his face pink, his eyes shooting sparks. By the time Montrose sent out their punting squad, he had started to shake like a chemical bomb about to explode.

As the offensive team set up, Calvin pranced like a prizefighter, until Cathy finally showed him the proper place to stand.

"This isn't going to work!" Boots whispered to Bruno. "We're going to have a dead Beast on our hands!"

As Cathy called the signals, there was a bone-chilling cry that had everyone looking to see if a Bengal tiger had somehow gotten onto the field. The ball was snapped, and Calvin took off as though he had been fired out of a rocket launcher. Screaming all the way, he hit Craig full in the stomach, bouncing off him like a rubber ball against a brick wall. Craig just stared at him in amazement.

Cathy took two steps back and found Dave Jackson with a pass. It was a very short throw, but the Maulers were completely unprepared. Dave took off on the dead run, and the defenders were too late in pursuit. He ran seventy-five yards for a touchdown.

The seven-man vacuum-cleaner tuba emitted an enormous blast that raised Miss Scrimmage to her feet to lead a standing ovation. Suddenly the home-made noisemakers were back in use, and the signs and banners were held high. Dave Jackson's father was so proud that his wife and children had to restrain him from running onto the field.

Calvin still lay in a heap on the ground where he'd bounced off Craig. Bruno jogged up, jubilant. "Way to go, Beast!"

Calvin didn't move. "I think I've got another compound fracture!"

"No, you don't! You're fine!"

"How do you know?" roared Calvin in outrage. "Are you a doctor?"

"No, but I've seen a lot of them on TV." Bruno reached out a hand. "Get up, Beast. We just scored a touchdown!"

"We did?"

"Yeah! You made the key hit. Listen to that cheering. That's for you."

"The Beast strikes again!" roared Calvin, scrambling to his feet. He charged to the sidelines, where Mr. Carson slapped him on the back so hard it almost knocked him over.

"They have no pass defense!" Mr. Klapper was yelling excitedly over the crowd noise. "They're used to Trolley doing it all for them! We're not out of this one yet!"

Douglas Greer arrived at Macdonald Hall on foot. There was nowhere to park anywhere near the school. He had to walk half a mile from his car before he reached the tree-lined south edge of the school grounds. There, irritated and a little tired, he found nobody around. The entire campus was deserted, except for the football stadium. He couldn't see the stadium beyond the Faculty Building, but the roar of the crowd was loud and clear. He remembered that Macdonald Hall was hosting the Daw Cup game today. All the better. It would be best to confront Klapper without many people around.

Following a sign indicating the direction of the spare cottage, he went over some possible opening

170

lines for when he met Klapper. Perhaps "Klapper, what the blue blazes . . . ?" Or something more subtle: "Klapper, I've known some stupid people in my life, but *you*. . . ." Then there was the sarcastic approach: "Kevin, what a surprise! I must thank you for that *wonderful* plant. . . ." Or the direct line: "Hey, idiot! You're fired!"

He found the cottage and rapped insistently on the door. It swung open. Greer took a tentative step inside. "Klapper?" he called. There was no response.

He peered into the kitchen and froze in horror. It looked like the aftermath of a rumble. A splatter of blood decorated the wall where Sidney had walked into it the night before. From there, a long smear led to a dried puddle on the floor. Stray drops were everywhere, as Sidney had scrambled around in search of ice and paper towels. The refrigerator was particularly hard-hit.

Eyes wide, Greer checked the living room. There was Klapper's briefcase. And his clothes were in the bedroom drawers. He was living here, all right. Brow furrowed, Greer sat down on the couch, resting his chin on his fist. What had happened?

Out of the corner of his eye, he caught sight of some Ministry of Education letterhead in the wastebasket. He could make out the title "Report to Curriculum Supervisor on Private School Macdonald Hall." Greer looked up in dismay. He'd never received this report! Breathlessly he grabbed the sheets and examined them. He found himself looking at a photocopy of Klapper's original report — dated the Friday before the deadline, over nine weeks ago. So Klapper *had* completed a report, and

171

right on time, too! Why hadn't he submitted it? Why had he gone underground? Greer began to read:

Macdonald Hall is a sad example of a fine school gone sour. This institution, once the cornerstone of private education in Canada, has sold out to the flashy advantages of a high-profile sports program. Football, the most obsessive of all sports. . . .

Urgently Greer began to skim the rest of the text, his face paling as he read. By the time he put down the pages, he was paralyzed with fear. Klapper had written a report on Macdonald Hall that would put a black mark on the most spotless of records. It all added up. *This* was why Sturgeon had refused to discuss Klapper on the phone! A school like Macdonald Hall would stop at nothing to save its reputation. But — *murder?* Had Klapper been eliminated to prevent him from submitting his report? It was unbelievable! And those crazy letters — they must have been secret messages from Klapper that Greer in his anger and annoyance hadn't understood. Poor Kevin!

Hands trembling, Greer reconnected the phone and dialed the police. He had to see justice done.

13.
The
Final
Touchdown

The crowd noise in the Macdonald Hall football stadium was a single uninterrupted roar. Coach Flynn spent the half talking to himself on the sidelines, saying "I can't believe he's doing it," over and over again. Calvin "The Beast" Fihzgart was completely shutting down Craig Trolley, the best junior-high-school player in Ontario. And he was doing it not by talent, strength, speed, or "smarts." He was going on pure guts.

Every play was identical. Calvin would take off at top speed and slam himself full-force against Craig's immense form. Then he would crumple to the ground, dazed. Craig was not affected in the least, except he was so bewildered by the ferocity of the smaller boy's attack that he would hesitate.

173

By the time he could continue his run at the quarterback, Cathy would have already completed a pass. Then Bruno and Boots would haul Calvin to his feet again, and set him up for the next play.

With Calvin paving the way, Cathy Burton was having the game of her life. The Maulers could not defend against her passing attack. Scoring two more third-quarter touchdowns, and allowing only one, the Warriors closed the gap to ten points, trailing 31–21.

The fourth quarter was end-to-end action. Macdonald Hall thundered downfield to cut the gap to three points, only to have the Maulers rebound and widen it back to ten. Again the Warriors scored, and again Montrose responded. With only two minutes and fifteen seconds remaining, Sidney Rampulsky caught a spectacular pass in the end zone to make the score Maulers 45, Warriors 42.

"The defense is exhausted!" exclaimed Coach Flynn. "We can't put some of these boys in again!"

"We'll play!" Bruno jumped up, pulling Boots up with him. "We're not tired!"

So it was that Bruno and Boots jogged out onto the field with what was left of a battered, overworked defense.

Boots was livid. "Not tired, eh? I'm just ready to drop down dead right here on the field, that's all!"

"Listen, Boots," lectured Bruno, "if we let them score here, we can forget the Daw Cup!"

"I've already forgotten the Daw Cup," grumbled Wilbur as the Warriors lined up. "I just want to go back to my room and sleep for a month!"

The play was a quick handoff, and Boots grabbed the ball carrier, but couldn't seem to finish the tackle. Bruno rammed his shoulder determinedly into the runner. The ball popped loose, rolling on the turf.

"*Fumble!*" bellowed Bruno.

Wilbur was there first, hurling himself onto the ball. It slipped out from under his weight, was kicked by many scrambling feet, bounced off a face mask, and landed right in the hands of Pete Anderson and one of the Maulers. They held a small tug-of-war, until Larry Wilson grabbed it from both of them, but dropped it. A gasp went up in the stadium as every one of the players sprinted after the careening ball. Bruno, unable to run another step, howled, "*Get it, Boots!*" and used what was left of his energy to push his roommate from behind. Boots lost his balance and flew forward, grasping madly for the ball. The entire Maulers team pounced on top of him. The crowd went wild.

"Great play, O'Neal!" commended Mr. Klapper as the Warriors gathered on the sidelines. "Okay, our whole season's just come down to the last two minutes. Are you ready?"

The three coaches surveyed their team. The Warriors were beaten up and tired. After a first half of disaster, and a second of grueling action, the question was: Did anyone have anything left to give?

"We're ready!" gasped Bruno.

Mr. Carson placed a beefy hand on Bruno's shoulder pad. "Get out there and do your best," he said very quietly.

All through the second half, the Mauler defense had been helpless against the Warriors, but Macdonald Hall was tiring just when the defending champions were catching their second wind. Agonizingly slowly, Cathy led the Warriors down the field, but the defense tightened with every play. It was nail-biting time for the almost silent crowd as Montrose Junior High dug in its heels. The offense was paralyzed as the time ticked away, and with it, the hopes of the home team. Finally with eight seconds to play, and the ball on the Maulers' 35-yard line, Mr. Klapper took the last Macdonald Hall time-out.

"We've had it!" declared Coach Flynn in a panic.

All at once, the players began to babble nervously.

Kevin Klapper raised his hands for order. "Listen up. I want all the receivers in the end zone. One of you will be getting a pass. Catch it."

As the players moved back onto the field, Klapper sidled up to Cathy. "Okay, Drimsdale," he whispered. "When their defense chases our guys into the end zone, tuck in the ball and run."

Cathy flashed him a thumbs-up, and jogged out to the huddle.

"Last play of the game, guys," said Bruno to the group as they lined up. "The honor of Macdonald Hall is at stake here."

There were grunts and mumbles. Everyone was concentrating too hard to speak. This was it. Zero hour.

Cathy took the snap and faded back. All at once, six Warriors charged for the end zone, running zig-zag patterns all over the field. The defenders raced after them.

"*Hey!*" called Craig Trolley. "Watch out for the — " The Beast hit him like a Polaris missile, right in the midsection. This time Calvin didn't bounce off. Pitching backward, Craig hit the ground like a ton of bricks. *"Oooooof!"*

The Maulers' linemen turned and stared in amazement. And by the time they looked back, Cathy Burton had stepped around them, and was in full flight for the goal line. Wheeling, they charged after her.

"Oh, no!" blurted Boots. He joined the stampede, shouting, *"Be careful!"*

"He's running it himself!" cried Carson. "What a play!"

Suddenly the Maulers in the end zone caught sight of Cathy, and realized there was no pass coming. In a wild effort to recover, they ran to stop her before she could get across the goal line.

In the stands, Diane grabbed the smelling salts from Miss Scrimmage and covered her eyes. "I can't look!"

"Don't be silly," laughed the Headmistress airily. "I'm sure young Drimsdale can take care of himself."

"That's not Elmer Drimsdale!" quavered Diane. "It's Catherine!"

"Catherine?" repeated Miss Scrimmage. "That's ridiculous! Catherine is right over — right over — " She let out an earsplitting shriek. "Great heavens! *Where's Catherine?*"

Cathy hugged the ball and ran as Maulers converged on her from all directions like ants towards a sugar cube. They all seemed to hit at the same time, and she disappeared under a rain of Montrose jerseys.

Referees, coaches, players, and spectators all stared at the pileup, half over the goal line. A nervous buzz went up in the stadium. The clock had run out. Where was the ball?

The referees tried to unscramble the mountain of bodies, but the Maulers' defenders refused to budge. Suddenly Miss Scrimmage burst onto the field, scrambling around like a flustered chicken. "Goodness!" she shrieked, running up to the goal line. *"Get off, you big brutes!"* She began pulling the Maulers bodily off the pileup. The officials watched her in amazement. When she yanked the last player away, there lay Cathy, tightly clutching the football, half an inch over the goal line.

The referee raised his arms and bellowed, "Touch — "

That was all he got out. As with one voice, a howl of joy rose over the stadium and hung there in the air. It was mingled with the sound of thousands of feet on wooden bleacher benches as Warrior supporters, in a body, rushed the field. The Macdonald Hall players stampeded to the fallen Cathy, and hoisted her up on their shoulders, in spite of Miss Scrimmage's efforts to get her back. Diane was there, too, screaming herself hoarse, and joining in the procession to the middle of the field. There huddled the three Macdonald Hall coaches, arms around each other, blubbering.

As the crowd hit the turf, a full-fledged mob scene ensued. The cheerleaders forgot their routines, and joined the general celebration. Some of the younger staff members dumped a bucket of water over Coach Flynn's head. The seven-man vacuum-cleaner tuba let out a blast that knocked Miss Scrimmage into the arms of Pete Anderson. Cathy hadn't stopped screaming since the referee had signaled her touchdown. She sounded very little like Elmer Drimsdale, but no one could tell in the overall roar. Seconds after the scoreboard registered 48–45, Macdonald Hall, a howling Mark Davies ran down to join the party.

"We won!" cried Boots in disbelief. "We actually won!"

He caught a sideways look from Bruno that clearly said, "Didn't I tell you this was going to happen?" The Warriors were aglow, but Bruno's face was the brightest of them all, shining like a jack-o'-lantern. It was he who started the chorus of "We Are the Champions," which caught on, and swelled to fill the stadium.

As team captain, Bruno was clutching the game ball, searching the crowd for the one player who deserved this above all others. Calvin Fihzgart, who had run around the field three times in an attempt to cool down, roared up, and Bruno held the ball out to him.

"Beast, this is for you. You've earned it."

Wildly Calvin grabbed the ball, held it like an ear of corn on the cob, and sank his teeth into the laces. There was a loud pop, and suddenly the game ball, the great honor, was flat as a pancake.

The crowd parted to make way for a man in a double-breasted blue blazer. In his arms he carried the Daw Cup, a large sterling-silver bowl on a polished wood pedestal. The three coaches began to bawl.

"On behalf of the Ontario Junior Sports Commission," the blue blazer bellowed, "I am pleased to present the Daw Cup to the captain of the champion Macdonald Hall Warriors!"

Bruno accepted the trophy as flashbulbs went off in all directions. He held it high over his head, then passed it to Mr. Carson. Carson kissed it reverently, and handed it to the drenched and shivering Coach Flynn. Flynn, in turn, placed it in the hands of Kevin Klapper.

"KE-VIN!"

Klapper jumped, fumbling the trophy in his arms, but hanging on for dear life. He looked up to see Marjorie pushing through the crowd, the children in tow.

"M-M-M-Marjorie? What are you doing here?"

"What am I doing here? What are you doing here? You gave up football, remember?"

Hastily Klapper handed the trophy back to Flynn. He smiled weakly. "Dear, I have a little confession to make."

The referee rushed over. "We can't end the game officially," he called to the three coaches, "until you kick the extra point."

"Sure," said Carson, still jubilant. "Where's Blankenship?"

Everyone looked around. The Macdonald Hall kicker was nowhere to be seen.

"Where's the Blabbermouth?" asked Bruno in annoyance. "We have to finish the game."

Suddenly a hush fell, and all eyes turned up to the scoreboard. There, in blazing lights, were the words:

** BRUNO WALTON HAS A LUCKY PENNY **

"That *Blabbermouth!*" exclaimed Bruno in horror. "He's got the scoreboard controls!"

Boots shook his head in amazement. "We made him promise not to blab stuff; but we never said he couldn't spell it out in lights!"

** GARY POTTS HAS DANDRUFF **
** HARVEY WILKINS IS AFRAID OF THE DARK **
** SHELDON BALSAM WRITES TO SANTA **
** CHRIS TALBOT HAS TOE COMPLICATIONS **

A ripple of laughter swept through the crowd.

Boots ran up to his quarterback. "Cathy," he whispered, "don't you think it's about time you swapped places with Elmer?"

"Oh, give me a break, will you? The season's over! Let me have a few more minutes of glory!"

** FRED BASS HAS BUNNY-RABBIT SLIPPERS **

At that moment, the sound of police sirens cut the air. The crowd fell silent. Everyone listened as the sirens came closer and closer. And then there was a new sound, a wild, high-pitched chattering, radiating from the north bleachers.

"Elmer's bush hamsters!" exclaimed Bruno in amazement.

"That's impossible!" cried Boots. "Four little animals couldn't be that loud!"

The sirens were right outside, howling, wailing, and the chattering sound rose to a crescendo. The north bleachers of the Macdonald Hall football stadium erupted in a tidal wave of gray-brown fur. A wall of out-of-control, gibbering Manchurian bush hamsters swept over the horrified crowd, swarming everywhere among the celebrants.

181

** TED WOLFE WAS IN DIAPER COMMERCIALS **

Screams rang out as the four hundred and fifty-one crazed animals bounced and scrambled around the field, fur standing rigidly on end. There was a stampede for the exits, but these were blocked by uniformed police officers.

Pete Anderson had finally managed to revive Miss Scrimmage when a bush hamster hit her full in the face and hung on, claws in her bouffant hair.

Kevin Klapper was bowled over in the rush of people, and borne away.

"Kevin, you come back here!" stormed his wife. "I haven't finished with you — "

Big Henry Carson snatched up Marjorie in one arm and the children in the other in an attempt to save them from the mad scramble.

"Put me down, you phony zucchini person!"

Karen sank her teeth into Carson's arm, and he dropped the three of them with a cry of pain.

** MICHAEL COX DOESN'T CHEW HIS FOOD **

A baby bush hamster crawled up Wilbur's jersey. With a scream of pure terror, the big boy ripped off his sweater, and brushed the animal away. Thinking this to be a gesture of victory, several of the other Warriors removed their shirts and tossed them high. Sidney attempted this as well, but could not get the shirt up over his head. He stumbled about blindly in the general confusion, bumping into Boots, who knocked over Bruno, who in turn cut the legs out from under Dave Jackson's father. The chain reaction continued until the field was a mass of wallowing arms and legs and bush hamsters.

In the locker room, Elmer ignored the noise at first, waiting anxiously for Cathy's arrival. Whatever cheering was going on was no doubt for him anyway. It meant Macdonald Hall had won, and he was a bigger hero than ever. He adjusted his silver-sequinned collar and dusted off his pink sneakers with a clean towel. Yes, he could hear police sirens. Good idea. Thousands of fans, all after quarterback Elmer Drimsdale, would have to be kept in order somehow.

But there was another sound — not police, and not ecstatic fans. It rose with the sirens — a high-pitched chattering. A familiar sound — the sound of — of —

"*Manchurian bush hamsters!*" he howled, leaping to his feet. Completely forgetting the plan, he charged out of the clubhouse and onto the field. His jaw dropped.

There was a full-fledged riot in progress, but Elmer saw nothing but his bush hamsters — dozens — no, *hundreds* of them. The bush hamsters had reproduced! On their own! But how? Hysterical with joy, he rushed into the melee, plowing through anyone who got in his way.

Sidney Rampulsky, his jersey still wrapped around his neck, ran up to him, holding an armload of four bush hamsters. "Here they are, Elmer," he announced proudly. "The four I lost." He frowned in perplexity. "I don't know where all these others came from."

At that moment, the wailing police sirens were

switched off, and instantly the four hundred and fifty-one bush hamsters settled down. The scene, which had seconds before been raucous pandemonium, was now tranquil. Cautiously staff, students, players, and officials got to their feet.

Elmer looked down. The baby bush hamster that had been clawing at his leg was now sedately munching on a half-eaten zucchini stick. Zucchini sticks! Of course!

Coach Flynn looked around to assure himself of the safety of his players. His eyes fell on Elmer, who stood at midfield, patting a bush hamster lovingly. He wheeled to regard number 00, quarterback Drimsdale, who, along with Bruno, was hoisting the Daw Cup. He turned back to Elmer, then to his quarterback again.

"Drimsdale!" he blurted, pointing downfield. "What are you doing over there? You're over *here*!"

Henry Carson followed the coach's pointing finger. He turned to Cathy. "Well, if that's Drimsdale — then who are *you*?"

Oh, no, thought Boots, as a curious circle formed around Cathy.

Reluctantly Cathy removed her helmet and glasses. Some of the bobby pins shook loose, and her long dark hair tumbled about her shoulder pads. She smiled weakly. "Hey, dudes."

A great gasp went up from the spectators. "A *girl?!*"

Within seconds, the message on the scoreboard read:

** OUR QUARTERBACK IS A GIRL **

184

Mrs. Sturgeon burst onto the scene. "Yes, and what a girl!" She grasped Cathy's hand earnestly. "Congratulations, dear! You were wonderful!"

"But a *girl* — ?!" exclaimed Mr. Carson, dumbfounded.

Haughtily the man in the blue blazer stepped up and grabbed the Daw Cup from Bruno's grasp. "Ineligible player! Macdonald Hall loses by default!"

A howl of protest went up in the stadium.

"Ineligible?!" bellowed Carson. "Whoever said girls can't play football?"

"Psst. You did," whispered Klapper. "*Sports Illustrated* interview, 1979."

"Well, what do *I* know? We won fair and square!"

Blue Blazer sniffed. "Oh, really? Is the girl a registered student of Macdonald Hall?"

"Sort of!" said Carson positively.

"She's one of *my* students!" shrilled Miss Scrimmage. "And she was coerced into doing this by that horrible man — " she pointed to Carson " — and the dreadful boys from Macdonald Hall, who have been terrorizing my innocent girls for years!"

"The truth comes out!" said Blue Blazer triumphantly.

Henry Carson snorted loudly. "Big deal! Everybody here saw our guys — and girl — win that championship! So as far as I'm concerned, you can take that stupid trophy, and — "

"Henry, that will do," came a familiar voice. Everyone turned to see Mr. Sturgeon standing there, his expression severe. "It is obvious that the Warriors deserve to be disqualified."

Blue Blazer nodded righteously.

Mr. Sturgeon fixed the league official with a cold,

fishy stare. "It is further obvious exactly which team won the championship game. The disposition of the trophy is irrelevant. Our Warriors — " He fell silent, and watched with everyone else as a line of police officers swept towards them.

Kevin Klapper's keen eyes made out the portly figure of Douglas Greer in their midst. "It's my boss!" he exclaimed to no one in particular. "With the cops!"

"Don't worry, Kevin," soothed Carson. "No one can be arrested for not showing up for work." He looked thoughtful. "At least, I don't *think* so."

The officers came closer, and suddenly Greer pointed a pudgy finger at Macdonald Hall's Headmaster. "There he is! That's Sturgeon! The bald one with the glasses!"

Bruno froze. "Oh, no!" he rasped to Boots. "We cheated to win the cup, and now they've come to arrest The Fish!"

Boots went white. "What are we going to do?"

A plainclothes officer flanked by two uniforms approached Mr. Sturgeon and flashed identification. "Sir, I'm Detective-Sergeant Flange. I'm going to have to ask you some questions."

Mr. Sturgeon was completely mystified. "About what?"

Bruno sprinted onto the scene and interposed himself dramatically between Flange and Mr. Sturgeon. "He didn't do anything! I'm the team captain! I'll take the rap!"

"Stand aside, Walton," said the Headmaster. "This doesn't concern you."

"Yes, it does, sir. I — I knew about Cathy right from the beginning." He turned to Flange and the officers. "We deliberately bent the rules so we could win the championship. It's all my fault."

"And mine," put in Boots in a squeaky voice.

Flange looked around. "Go away, kids. I'm trying to conduct an investigation into the disappearance of Kevin Klapper."

Klapper snapped to attention. "Me?"

For the first time, Greer spotted him, and broke into a wide smile. "Kevin! You're alive!" The smile faded abruptly. *"I'll kill you!"* He approached menacingly, but Marjorie got in his way.

"Get in line!" she growled, and turned to face her husband. "Kevin, you promised me that never again would you have anything to do with football!"

Greer butted in. "Klapper, do you have any idea of the trouble you've caused? You don't just walk out on a job for nine weeks!"

"What about your career?" Marjorie thundered. "And your family! If you can't think about me, think about the children!"

"We don't mind," piped Kevin, Jr.

Flange looked confused. "If this guy's Klapper, and he's safe and sound, whose blood was splattered all over the kitchen in that cottage?"

Sidney raised his hand. "That was mine. I'm a bleeder."

Greer was still roaring. "And ruining your life is your own business! But you made me look like an idiot! Why didn't you just call me and say, 'Greer, I've gone crazy. I'm quitting my job'? That I would have understood! Now I'm mad at you, your wife's mad at you, and the police are mad at you, too!"

Flange drew himself up tall. "No, Mr. Greer. We're mad at *you*. We don't appreciate murder investigations with no victim. Our time is valuable, so if you have no more homicides for us to check out, we'll be going."

Greer glared at Klapper. "Now I'm *twice* as mad at you, because the cops are mad at *me!*"

Marjorie snorted. "You're mad? How about broken promises? He's a bum — "

Henry Carson drew himself up to his considerable height, thrust out an enormous palm, and said, "Cool it! I refuse to listen to another bad thing about Kevin." He put an arm around Klapper's narrow shoulders. "This man knows more about football than anyone I've ever seen! To say he blew it as a curriculum inspector is like telling Albert Einstein he's a lousy short-order cook! Forcing him to ignore football is nuts! Kevin, the coaching spot is opening up next year at Belvedere U., where I played my college ball. I talked the athletic director into giving you an interview, and you're a cinch for the job!"

Klapper's face lit up like a Christmas tree.

"It pays a bundle," Carson went on. "But let me tell you, Kevin, it's only the beginning. I *know* one day I'm going to see you coaching in the Super Bowl!"

The cheer that followed came from every heart.

The Montrose Junior High Maulers, league champions still, left with their trophy soon after. None of the Macdonald Hall supporters seemed to mind. "We won," was the message they took home with them, undaunted by who had the Daw Cup. The police and Mr. Greer left, too, and Miss Scrimmage collected her girls, Cathy included, and whisked them home.

After nearly eleven weeks of residence, Kevin Klapper moved out of the spare cottage, and packed his belongings into the family car. The entire team was there to see him off, and he kissed every single one of them, the coaches, and even Mrs. Sturgeon. Marjorie did, too, happy again, and looking forward to a new life at Belvedere U.

About a quarter mile down the road, a large sign blocked traffic: ALL BRILLIANT FOOTBALL COACHES STOP HERE. Cathy Burton and a small delegation of girls waited there, with a dozen roses to speed Mr. Klapper on his way.

It was almost dark as Coach Flynn poked his head in through the stadium entrance and called out to the last Warrior left on the field.

"Fihzgart, are you still here?"

"Just winding down, Coach," replied Calvin, folding up the squashed game ball and tucking it away in his hip pocket.

"Go get your dinner, Fihzgart. They're going to close the kitchen soon. No more laps, okay?"

Calvin joined his coach, and they headed for the dining hall. "There are a lot of memories on that field," he said philosophically.

"You only played half a game," the coach pointed out gently.

"Yeah, but with The Beast, it's intense."

Flynn nodded, remembering the boy's almost unbelievable courage. "A week ago, I would have given you an argument, but not today. You are everything you ever claimed to be — rough, tough, and mean. You were magnificent, Beast. It's really a shame you have to hang up your cleats today. Your beasting career is over for the year."

Calvin stared at him, eyes afire against the deep blue of the night. "Are you kidding? Hockey season starts this week! And do you know who's the roughest, toughest, meanest defenseman on skates?"

Flynn held his head. "I've got a pretty good idea."

14.
The
All-You-Can-Eat
Deluxe
Zucchini
Kitchen

Mr. Sturgeon's lecture on cheating was loud and long. Bruno and Boots sat shamefaced on the bench in his office, bitter in the knowledge that, across the road, Cathy Burton was being treated as the victim. As the Headmaster spoke of honor, ethics, and integrity, Bruno was thinking only of stupidity. Yesterday, believing Mr. Sturgeon was under arrest for their cheating, he had opened up his mouth and confessed to the wrong crime!

Mr. Sturgeon leaned forward and fixed them with his steely gray gaze. "I hope you boys realize that, if you had played with a legitimate all-Macdonald-Hall team, you would not have had your trophy taken away and your championship revoked."

"Yes, sir," said Bruno earnestly, "except that,

without Cathy, we would have been in last place."

Mr. Sturgeon smiled thinly. "Yes, I suppose you're right. She was rather — proficient. But don't sell yourselves short. The Macdonald Hall players worked very hard, and achieved a great deal on their own. This institution is proud of you. And ashamed," he added hastily.

"Thank you, sir," said Boots, frowning.

"As to the participation of Miss Burton," the Headmaster went on, "we will say nothing, as we all know Miss Burton. One neither coerces nor stops that young woman. She is a law unto herself."

The two boys stared at the carpet and said nothing.

"And since the football season is over, and will not start again for a year, I am inclined to be lenient with you. However, you will give me your word that you will *never* do anything like this again."

"I promise," chorused Bruno and Boots readily.

"And you will clean up the stadium. The little fracas that followed yesterday's game has left rather a mess. Parts of the field and bleachers need repair, and there is a goodly amount of garbage and zucchini sticks in the area. As for the bush hamster nest under the north stands — the janitorial staff will supply you with shovels. Feel free to recruit other guilty parties to assist you in this endeavor."

Bruno and Boots exchanged agonized glances.

The door opened, and Henry Carson peered in. "Mr. Sturgeon?" He caught sight of Bruno and Boots, and broke into a wide grin. "Hi, champs."

Mr. Sturgeon regarded him with distaste. "The reason we have a waiting area is so that one may wait."

192

"Oh, that's okay," said Carson jovially. "Walton and O'Neal can stay. This concerns them, too." He established himself in a visitor's chair. "I came to tell you that I'm a man of my word. I want you to know that I don't buy this disqualification garbage one bit. *We* won the Daw Cup. I promised the men a rec hall for a good showing, and now I'm ready to deliver."

Mr. Sturgeon sighed. "Carson, this is hardly the time for rewards. I have been trying to impress upon Walton and O'Neal that cheating is unacceptable."

"Aw, come on, sir," Mr. Carson wheedled. "You and I both know the school's planning to build them a rec hall anyway. Let me build it and put in a few extra items to make it really special — as a thank-you to the guys for giving me the most fun I've had since I graduated from Macdonald Hall."

The Headmaster groaned. "What is your proposal?"

From his pocket, Mr. Carson produced a crumpled piece of paper and unfolded it before them. "I made a little sketch last night. Let me know what you think." He snatched up a pencil and began to point out the various features. "Here we've got a wide-screen TV, VCR, and stereo, with a bunch of beanbag chairs over here. We can put some video games across this wall. The fireplace goes in beside the Ping-Pong and the pool tables, but far enough from the soft drink and candy machines so that people aren't bumping into each other. Okay so far?"

"Beautiful!" breathed Bruno in ecstasy.

"Fantastic!" echoed Boots.

"Good," said Carson, continuing. "Now, here's the other part. Another TV, regular size, lots of couches and tables by the library leading into the cafe-style area off the all-you-can-eat deluxe zucchini kitchen."

Bruno and Boots exchanged a look of sheer horror. No. Not that. A beautiful rec hall, a dream rec hall, the *ultimate* rec hall, and it had to have zucchini sticks.

"Mr. Carson," began Bruno painfully, "we've talked it over with the guys — " He bit his tongue. When they heard about the zucchini kitchen, the guys would forgive him for this. "You've done so much for us already — the stadium, the team, the equipment. But most of all, you've been a real friend."

"That's right," said Boots. "We just can't accept anything more from you."

"But thanks for the thought," added Bruno in a strangled voice.

Henry Carson was deeply touched. "I'm all choked up, men."

Mr. Sturgeon smiled. "I think this has gone far enough, gentlemen. Walton, O'Neal, you have something to tell Mr. Carson, something that should have been said right at the beginning. The fact is, you love his recreation hall, *but* — " he prompted.

"We hate your zucchini sticks," Bruno barely whispered.

"Pardon?"

"We hate your zucchini sticks!" chorused Bruno and Boots.

Mr. Carson looked startled. "Everybody?"

Mr. Sturgeon supplied the answer. "To a man."

"Well, why didn't you just say something?"

194

"We didn't want to hurt your feelings," said Bruno.

Carson was thunderstruck. "But you ate so many!"

Bruno hung his head. "We flushed them, we threw them in the woods, we buried them, and we fed the rest to the bush hamsters. You weren't supposed to find out. We didn't eat any at all."

"But I wouldn't have cared!"

Both boys looked at him in amazement.

Henry Carson grinned. "You've never seen *me* eating one of those things, have you? Yuccchh!"

Bruno and Boots left the Faculty Building on the run.

"I can't believe it!" howled Boots. "All that zucchini disposal — for nothing!"

"Don't complain, Melvin," Bruno puffed. "A championship yesterday, and the ultimate rec hall today — *minus* the zucchini kitchen."

They were running to the spot on the front driveway where a truck from Environment Canada was just about to leave with Elmer's four hundred and fifty-one Manchurian bush hamsters. A small crowd of boys had gathered to see off the animals that had so livened up the Daw Cup game.

Elmer was standing by the driver's door, making the man write down the recipe for Mr. Zucchini batter.

"It kind of makes you feel important," said Pete Anderson. "Our school saved the Manchurian bush hamster."

"I'm going to miss those little guys," sighed Wil-

195

bur as the truck drove off. "Could they ever eat!"

The boys all waved the bush hamsters out of sight.

"Great news, guys!" piped Bruno suddenly. "We're getting our rec hall, and it's going to have *everything!*"

There were oohs and ahs as Bruno and Boots began listing the marvelous facilities the hall would include.

"And here's the bad news," Boots continued. "We have to clean up the stadium."

The excitement ended abruptly.

"Define 'we,' " said Wilbur.

"We," said Bruno. "Us. All the guys. It's The Fish's punishment for the Cathy thing. Kind of a drag but, face it, it could have been a lot worse."

"Oh, yeah?" challenged Larry. "Have you seen the stadium? It looks like a garbage dump! And then, *under* the north bleachers — "

"Come on, guys," coaxed Bruno. "We won the championship; now it's time to pay our dues."

"I don't want to do this," complained Sidney.

"All right, everybody," said Bruno, beginning to herd them in the direction of the stadium. "Let's go, Pete. Move it out, Dave. That's the way, Blabbermouth. Don't worry. It'll all be over in a few hours."

With much grumbling, the group headed off towards the north lawn. Bruno regarded the lone figure still standing by the driveway. "Shake a leg, Elm. You're in this, too." He watched as Elmer produced a piece of paper from his back pocket, unfolded it lovingly, and held it out.

It was Elmer's contract with Bruno, signed the

day before the road trip to Kingston. He waved it confidently.

"Aw, Elm, that was weeks ago! You're not going to hold me to it, are you?"

Whistling, Elmer started off towards the dormitories.

"Come back here! I signed that thing under pressure!"

From the stadium, Wilbur Hackenschleimer's voice called, "Hey, Walton! Get over here and do some work!"

Bruno didn't hear him. "Talk about gratitude!" he bawled at Elmer's receding back. "If I hadn't started using your stupid rats for zucchini disposal, there'd still be four of them today!"

Without turning around, Elmer waved his contract over his shoulder, and kept on walking.

"I hope your helium experiment turns to sewer gas!" roared Bruno. Elmer did not flinch. "Drimsdale! You'll never get away with this!"

Elmer turned a corner, walking out of view, leaving Bruno ranting at thin air.

APPENDIX

DELICIOUS MR. ZUCCHINI™ ZUCCHINI STICKS

Ingredients

1 lb. fresh zucchini, cut in spears
8 oz. Mr. Zucchini™ batter (now available in su-
permarkets everywhere)
2 cups vegetable oil

Method

Dip zucchini in batter until thickly coated. Deep fry in oil. Zucchini is ready when batter is golden brown. Serve with Mr. Zucchini Sweet-and-Sour, Blue Cheese, or Hot Mustard Dressing (now available in your grocer's freezer).

Serves 4

WARNING:
Do not feed to Manchurian bush hamsters.